## ABOUT THE AUTHOR

Barbara Cartland, the world's most famous romantic novelist, who is also an historian, playwright, lecturer, political speaker and television personality, has now written over 440 books and sold over 400 million all over the world.

She has also had many historical works published and has written four autobiographies as well as the biographies of her mother and that of her brother, Ronald Cartland, who was the first Member of Parliament to be killed in the last war. This book has a preface by Sir Winston Churchill and has just been republished with an introduction by Sir Arthur Bryant.

"Love at the Helm" a novel written with the help and inspiration of the late Earl Mountbatten of Burma, Great Uncle of His Royal Highness The Prince of Wales, is being sold for the Mountbatten Memorial Trust.

Miss Cartland in 1978 sang an Album of Love Songs with the Royal Philharmonic Orchestra.

In 1976 by writing twenty-one books, she broke the world record and has continued for the following nine years with 24, 20, 23, 24, 24, 25, 22, 26, and 25. In the Guinness Book of Records she is listed as the world's top-selling author.

In private life Barbara Cartland, who is a Dame of Grace of the Order of St. John of Jerusalem, Chairman of the St. John Council in Hertfordshire and Deputy President of the St. John Ambulance Brigade, has fought for better conditions and salaries for Midwives and Nurses.

She has championed the cause for old people, had the law altered regarding gypsies and founded the first Romany Gypsy Camp in the world.

Barbara Cartland is deeply interested in Vitamin Therapy, and is President of the National Association for Health.

Her designs "Decorating with Love" are being sold all over the U.S.A. and the National Home Fashions League made her in 1981, "Woman of Achievement".

Barbara Cartland's book "Getting Older, Growing Younger", and her cookery book "The Romance of Food" have been published in Great Britain, the U.S.A. and in the rest of the world.

She has also written a Children's Pop-Up Book entitled "Princess to the Rescue".

In 1984 she received at Kennedy Airport, America's Bishop Wright Air Industry Award for her contribution to the development of aviation when in 1931 she and two R.A.F. Officers thought of, and carried, the first aeroplane-towed glider air-mail.

An experiment is taking place with Miss Cartland at the moment which has never happened with any author before.

Eagle Moss (Patrick Cavendish) is bringing out a hardback book every fortnight at £1.95p. Beautifully bound in red and gold leather it will make a Barbara Cartland Library.

## A CIRCUS FOR LOVE

Thelma, the daughter of Lord Fernhurst, overhears her Step-mother telling her lover, the penniless Sir Richard Leith, that Thelma's Great-Aunt has died and left her an enormous fortune.

Lady Fernhurst suggests that Sir Richard should marry the girl so that they can get their hands on her money.

Terrified that she will be unable to avoid being forced up the aisle, Thelma runs away, taking with her Watkins the batman of her brother who had been killed at Waterloo.

She had managed to collect enough money to keep her for some time and changes her name to Forde, having no idea where she is going.

On the second day after leaving home she sees a magnificent house in the distance and rides down the drive to look at it more closely.

To her surprise, she sees not far from the house the Big Top of a Circus with a tiger being taken on a lead into a cage.

Because she is curious she enters the tent and encounters the handsome Earl of Merstone, who has just returned from the Army of Occupation in France.

How Thelma finds the inside of the house is very different from how it appears outside, how she learns that the Earl is staging a Circus to raise enough money to save him from having to destroy his private menagerie and how she not only saves his life but also loses her heart, is told in this exciting 418th book by BARBARA CARTLAND.

BARBARA CARTLAND

# A CIRCUS FOR LOVE

Pan Original
Pan Books London and Sydney

First published 1987 by Pan Books Ltd
Cavaye Place, London SW10 9PG
9 8 7 6 5 4 3 2 1
© Cartland Promotions 1987
ISBN 0 330 29928 X
Printed in Great Britain by
Richard Clay Ltd, Bungay, Suffolk

# Author's Note

The Tower Menagerie was the most important collection of animals in Britain from a very early age.

The entrance fee was at first a penny or if preferred one could bring in a live dog or cat to give as food for the animals.

Lions were always the chief attraction and in the days of Elizabeth I were all named after Kings and Queens.

Towards the end of the seventeenth century the first hyena was shown in England and in 1739 a rhinoceros from Bengal.

William IV closed the menagerie after six-hundred years of unbroken history, and the animals went either to the Zoo or to Windsor.

The London Zoo, originated by Sir Stamford Raffles opened in April 1826. It was to become an example to the whole world, and every country in Europe began to copy it.

Private menageries have existed for centuries.

Julius Caesar mentioned in his Commentaries that rich English landlords had parks in which they kept hares, geese and chickens, not for eating, but almost as pets.

The Norman Lords who came over with William the Conqueror appropriated parks such as these for stocking with deer for the chase, and sometimes with less common animals also.

There is a record of a nobleman receiving a bear from William Rufus, and Henry I had at Woodstock, lions, leopards, lynxes and other animals.

In 1234 Henry III was sent by his son-in-law King Louis XIX of France a present of the first elephant ever seen in England.

At the Tower Menagerie when George IV came to the throne there was only one elephant, one grizzly bear and a few birds. By the end of the reign however the menagerie was very well stocked.

# Chapter One
# 1818

Thelma, riding back home through the Spring sunshine, thought that her father's house in the distance looked very attractive.

It was originally a Tudor Manor which had been enlarged over the generations and had housed the Fern family for three-hundred years.

The present Lord Fernhurst had been shattered when his only son was killed at Waterloo.

He had then given up being interested in his estate and spent much of his time in London.

The result was disastrous.

This time he had returned to the country at the beginning of the year, having married a woman whom Thelma had disliked on sight.

The feeling was mutual.

The new Lady Fernhurst had done everything within her power to make her Stepdaughter's life a misery.

At first Thelma had thought her father would be reasonable.

She was sure he would understand how difficult it was for her to see somebody strange taking her mother's place.

But Lord Fernhurst took the line of least resistance.

He had consoled himself for the loss of his first wife and for the vagaries of his second by drinking.

It was incredible to Thelma that her father should alter so completely in so short a time.

She had thought when first he had drunk so much after her brother's death that it was a temporary palliative.

She was sure he would soon be his normal self.

In London however he spent his time in his Club where they drank a great deal. Also in other places which she had heard encouraged drunkenness.

When after his last absence of nearly six months he returned to the country, it was difficult for Thelma to recognise him.

After her mother's death she had gone to a Finishing School.

It was when she came home for good that she found everything had changed, especially her father.

There was no doubt that Denise Fernhurst herself also encouraged him to drink.

This, Thelma thought scornfully, was so that he would not be aware of her outrageous behaviour.

She had never thought it possible that any lady could behave so badly.

She would have been very stupid if she had not been aware that her Stepmother had a lover.

In fact there had been two since she came home. While she gathered from what she had heard the servants saying, there had been several previous to that.

She was definitely shocked, and that was to put it mildly.

Her mother had been sweet, gentle, and very much in love with her father.

Thelma had therefore never come in contact with women like her Stepmother.

Denise was beautiful – no-one could deny that – but she was hard, avaricious and entirely pre-occupied with herself.

She was disagreeable to the elderly servants who had been at the Manor for years.

She would not call on the farmers on the Estate, or the old people in the village.

She disparaged them at mealtimes, which meant that what she said was repeated all over the Estate.

At first Lord Fernhurst was obviously infatuated with her, and it was clear that she could twist him round her little finger.

Then, Thelma thought, her father began to realise how unpleasant she was and to prevent himself from acknowledging the thought, he turned again to drink.

Thelma drew nearer to the house. She was riding one of the spirited horses from her father's stable.

She felt herself shrink inside at the thought that in a few minutes she would be in the company of her Stepmother.

At the same time, the thought of leaving home was appalling. It would be good-bye to everything that was familiar.

She supposed there were cousins, or perhaps one of her mother's sisters, who would look after her if she appealed to them.

Then a pride which was very much part of the family rose in her.

It made her feel it would be degrading to explain what had happened to her father.

The groom accompanying her out riding came to her side as they reached the courtyard.

He reached out to take the bridle of her horse as Thelma dismounted.

Once on the ground, she patted the horse's neck and he nuzzled against her.

Then she knew that she could not leave the horses she loved.

However unpleasant her Stepmother might be, there was always the relief of being able to ride away from the house.

At least for the time being she was out of reach of her bitter, sarcastic tongue.

"Thank you, Ben," Thelma said to the groom.

She walked up the ancient stone steps and into the oak-panelled hall.

She took off her riding-hat and put it with her gloves down on a chair.

As she glanced at the clock she realised she was later than usual, so she decided to have breakfast first before she changed into a gown.

She walked along the corridor that led to the Breakfast-Room. Looking out over the gardens, it caught the early-morning sun.

As she put out her hand to open the door she heard her name mentioned in her Stepmother's voice.

"How could we have imagined for one moment," she was saying, "that Thelma would be left so much money?"

"She is a very lucky girl!" a man's voice answered.

Thelma knew it was her Stepmother's lover speaking.

His name was Sir Richard Leith, and she had disliked him when he first arrived at the Manor three months ago.

"We will have to be clever about this," Denise Fernhurst said.

"Clever?" Sir Richard enquired.

He sounded curious, but not particularly interested.

"Do not be foolish!" Lady Fernhurst said sharply. "We want to get our hands on that money – at least you do!"

"You do not know what you are saying!" Sir Richard replied.

Denise Fernhurst's voice dropped to a lower note and Thelma guessed she was bending across the table towards him.

"Listen," she said, "the first thing we have to do is to prevent Thelma from seeing the newspapers. Secondly, you will leave at once for Canterbury."

"What for?" Sir Richard asked in a bewildered tone.

"Because, my dearest Darling, this is the opportunity for which you have been praying! You want money, and now we know Thelma has it!"

"Are you saying – are you suggesting – ?" Sir Richard began.

"I am telling you that you must marry the girl immediately before the fortune-hunters arrive to push you out of the way!"

Sir Richard was obviously stunned into silence, and Denise Fernhurst went on:

"Just think, when all that money is yours we can enjoy ourselves as we have never been able to do while I have to go down on my knees and beg for every penny!"

She made a little sound of delight before she went on:

"You can have everything you have always wanted: a place in London where we can be together, horses, phaetons, and clothes that will be the envy of every Beau in St. James's!"

'Denise, you are a genius!' Sir Richard exclaimed.

"I have always thought so,' Lady Fernhurst agreed complacently, "but it is a question of moving quickly before Thelma and that drunken fool to whom I am married realise what has happened.'

"Shall I speak to Thelma at once?" Sir Richard enquired.

"No, of course not!" Denise Fernhurst replied. "Say nothing until you have the Special Licence in your hands. Then I will force her to marry you before the Solicitors can inform her what is in the Will."

Thelma did not wait to hear any more.

She knew she had to see the newspapers which her Stepmother would hide from her.

She ran as swiftly and as silently as she could across the hall. At the end of another passage there was her father's Study.

She knew she would find there on the stool in front of the fireplace a newspaper.

Every morning old Newman the Butler, as he had done for the last thirty years, put the *Morning Post* on the breakfast-table and *The Times* in her father's Study.

Thelma opened the Study door.

She ran to where she saw *The Times* laid out with some magazines on the stool and picked it up.

She looked towards her father's desk.

As usual there was a pile of letters which would later be sorted out by Mr. Simpson the Estate Agent when he arrived.

Thelma had often thought it would be far easier and more convenient to put her father's mail, which he never looked at, directly into the Estate Office.

But that went against tradition, and Newman would never swerve from the duties he had always carried out punctiliously.

Thelma turned over the letters until she found what she was seeking.

It was quite obvious, she thought, that it came from a firm of Solicitors.

Their name was printed on the back of the envelope: *Marlow, Thestlethwaite and Downing*.

She slipped it into the pocket of her jacket, then she walked to the door she had left open.

She did not pass through it, but stood behind it and opened *The Times*, searching for what she expected to find.

It was on the second page and printed quite clearly.

It began:

*"DEATH OF THE DOWAGER DUCHESS OF WINTERTON."*

*"We deeply regret to announce the death of the Dowager Duchess of Winterton at the age of ninety-eight. The Duchess, who was an hereditary Lady-of-the-Bedchamber to Her Majesty the Queen, had been ill for some*

*years. She died peacefully in her country home in Northamptonshire.''*

It went on to describe how the Duchess had been the daughter of the 4th Lord Fernhurst and had married the Duke of Winterton when she was eighteen.

He had been the second son of the Duke of Winterton, and when his brother died, he became the heir and eventually the second Duke.

Then followed a long list of the charities of which the Duchess had been a patron, the many positions she had held of importance, and the honours she had received.

It continued:

*"The Duchess inherited a large fortune through her God-father, Sir Trevor Hayton, who was adviser to several Eastern Potentates. He never married but came back to England leaving on his death everything he possessed to his Godchild.*

*"It is understood that the Dowager Duchess has left her fortune to her great-niece, the Honourable Thelma Fern, who is the only daughter of the 6th Lord Fernhurst."*

Having read the report quickly, Thelma refolded *The Times* and put it back on the stool from where she had taken it.

Then she hurried quickly back to the Breakfast-Room.

She opened the door and instantly her Stepmother and Sir Richard, who had been still talking in low voices, were silent.

They both looked at her in a manner she would have thought strange had she not understood all too clearly the reason for it.

"Good-morning, Stepmother!" she said brightly.

"Good-morning, Sir Richard!"

They made no response.

She went to the sideboard to choose what to eat from the silver dishes which stood there with lighted candles beneath them to keep the food warm.

Then she sat down at the table saying as she did so:

"I am sorry if I am late, but it was so lovely riding in the sunshine that I went further than usual."

"I am glad you enjoyed it, dear," Lady Fernhurst said in a much more pleasant voice than she normally used.

As she spoke she flashed Sir Richard a meaningful glance, and he rose from the table.

"I had better be on my way," he said. "I hope you will not mind if I borrow a Phaeton from you, and a team of your excellent horses?"

"No, of course not," Lady Fernhurst said, "and try not to be late for dinner."

"Where is Sir Richard going?" Thelma asked in an innocent tone as he walked towards the door.

"He is going to visit some friends," her Stepmother replied vaguely.

Thelma was aware that Sir Richard looked back before he left the room and a glance passed between him and her Stepmother which was very revealing.

She pretended however to see nothing.

'How is Papa this morning?" she asked, as she filled her cup from the silver coffee-pot.

"Your father is asleep," Lady Fernhurst replied, "and do not wake him."

"No, of course not!" Thelma answered.

Lady Fernhurst rose to her feet holding the *Morning Post* tightly in her hand.

"I am sure you have plenty to do, Thelma," she said, "and I will be rather busy this morning."

"I understand," Thelma replied, "and I will be busy too."

16

She thought of the old adage as her Stepmother left the room: 'Many a true word spoken in jest'. It was very pertinent.

She had a great deal to do, and not much time in which to do it.

She finished her breakfast and hurried up the stairs.

As she went she was making a note in her mind of the things she required.

She went into her bed-room and found the maids had already tidied and cleaned it. She shut the door and sat down so that she could think clearly.

She knew that she had to leave home.

She was far too intelligent not to realise what would happen.

Her Stepmother would make it impossible for her to refuse to marry Sir Richard Leith.

She was only eighteen. That meant that by Law her father was her Guardian and whatever he decided she had to obey him.

She knew that when he was drunk her Stepmother could twist him into agreeing to anything she wanted.

She had already spent, Thelma knew, far more money than he could afford and he had even mortgaged part of the estate that was not entailed so that she could have more.

She would have sold the pictures if it had not been impossible.

They were in trust for whoever succeeded her father. Unless he had another son, this would be a nephew whom he had never liked.

Thelma knew that the idea of gaining a fortune would be irresistible to her Stepmother.

She would use any means in her power, however degrading, to get it into her clutches.

Only she could have thought of a plan so appalling as marrying her Stepdaughter to her penniless lover.

Sir Richard had conducted himself in a way that Thelma

thought was humiliating and outrageous.

When her father was sober enough to understand what was being said, Sir Richard 'toadied' to him.

He would flatter and compliment Lord Fernhurst.

Then as soon as he had staggered, or been carried off, to bed, he would snigger about him to her Stepmother.

"I hate him!" Thelma said to herself. "He is despicable."

She knew as she spoke that she would rather die than be married to such a man.

It was difficult to make up her mind where she should go.

She must hide somewhere where she could not be found and before Sir Richard returned to the Manor with the Special Licence.

She guessed that one of the things her Stepmother was doing at this moment was preparing the Chapel.

Built at the same time as the house, it was very beautiful.

Thelma always thought it was redolent with the faith of those who had devoutly worshipped in it.

When her mother was alive, her father's personal Chaplain, who was also the Vicar of the Church in the village, would come to the Manor every Sunday.

He would conduct a Service for all those who worked in the house or were staying in it.

The Services, which Thelma had known since she was a small girl, had always seemed very beautiful.

She had appreciated that everybody present was in a way part of the family.

The older servants always thought of the Manor as belonging to them.

They had revered her father and mother as their parents had.

They had loved Thelma and her brother Ivan because they had known them since they were born.

The new Lady Fernhurst quickly altered all that.

She abolished the Services, saying that the servants were

wasting their time when they should be working.

If her father had protested, Thelma had not heard him.

She only knew that the Chapel had been shut. The gardeners no longer put flowers on the altar, and the dust accumulated on the floor and on the carvings in the Chancel.

'It will take some time to get it clean,' she thought, and time was what she needed.

She took down several gowns from her wardrobe, choosing those that were of fine muslin or gauze.

They weighed nothing and could be packed into a very small space.

She put them on her bed and added nightgowns and other necessities.

She included a pair of satin slippers.

There was quite a pile when she had finished, but she knew it was not too much to be carried on two horses.

Years ago, when she had first gone to stay with some friends of her own age, her mother had bought her a pannier for her saddle.

Thelma remembered it was in a drawer in her bed-room.

She laid it out on her bed and filled the bags with the smaller things she had accumulated.

The gowns she rolled up and put into a long bag which would be fixed at the back of her saddle.

She then hid everything under her bed and walked down the stairs.

The most important and difficult thing was to make sure she had enough money. It would have to last her for a long time.

While she was thinking of what she should do, she remembered that to-morrow was Friday, and the last day of the month.

This meant that Mr. Simpson would be paying wages to everybody in the house and on the Estate. He would also have collected the money this morning from the Bank.

He would by now have returned, and would be attending to her father's letters.

After that she knew he would visit the farms to receive the rents from the farmers.

Then there were also the tenants who lived in their houses in the village.

This would take him until late in the afternoon.

She walked down to the Estate Office and saw it was empty.

She was sure that by this time Mr. Simpson would be riding from farm to farm. Some of them were a considerable distance from the Manor.

The monies he had brought from the Bank would be in the safe.

Locking the door of the Office so that no-one would be able to surprise her, Thelma found the key.

It was kept in what Mr. Simpson believed was a secret place, and she opened the safe.

As she expected, the money was there in neat little bags. One bag contained sovereigns, another half-sovereigns, a third silver.

What was more interesting was that there were a number of notes of much higher denominations.

These, Thelma knew, were used mostly by her father who disliked carrying anything bulky in his pockets.

She counted the notes quickly and found to her delight they amounted to over £100.

She put them in the pocket of her jacket, and took also the bags of money.

Looking a little further into the safe she found her father's cheque-book.

For a moment she hesitated.

She had no wish to do anything that could be held against her in a Court of Law, although it was unlikely she would be taken to one.

She had on several occasions in the last months written her father's name for him when he had been incapable of doing it himself.

Her Stepmother always refused to help anyone in the village.

Thelma had gone in despair to her father when some of the older servants who had served them for years were in desperate straits.

"Surely, Papa," she had pleaded, "you will help old Lucy, she was housemaid here for years. Now she needs a crutch so that she can move about, but she has no money with which to buy one."

"Of course, of course!" her father had said in a thick voice. "I will pay for it."

"I thought you would, Papa," Thelma said, "and there is Browning who used to stoke the boilers. He is almost blind and needs some spectacles."

She went on to read out a whole list of things that were required. She wrote out a cheque for them which came to quite a considerable sum.

Only when Lord Fernhurst came to sign the cheque did she realise his hand was shaking so badly that it was impossible.

She tried to guide him, but it was still no use.

Finally she signed the cheque herself, then showed him what she had done.

"That is your signature, is it not, Papa?" she asked.

"Yes – of course it – is," he said thickly.

Mr. Simpson had taken it to the Bank, and there had been no trouble about it.

She told herself now that if she was really desperate, she could forge her father's signature, and she was sure it would be honoured.

She therefore took two cheques from his cheque-book and put them in her pocket.

Then she wrote a note to Mr. Simpson, telling him what

money she had taken, and asked him to tell her father, but not her Stepmother.

She left the note in the safe and went back upstairs to her bed-room.

As she did so she saw maid-servants scurrying with brooms, buckets and brushes along the passage which led to the Chapel.

She guessed that her Stepmother was still there.

She then changed into her best riding-habit which had only recently arrived from London.

It was what her father had given to her as a birthday present.

He had been in one of his good moods and he had told her to go to the best-known tailor of ladies' riding-habits who was patronised by all the Ladies who belonged to the *Beau Ton*.

It was a very pretty habit in dark blue.

It made her hair look as golden as the Spring sunshine, and her skin as translucent as a pearl.

Underneath the full skirt she wore a starched petticoat edged with lace.

Her pretty blouse of fine muslin was inset with bands of lace.

The riding-hat, which she had bought at the same time, was very elegant with a gauze veil which matched her eyes and fluttered out behind when she was riding fast.

She also changed her riding-boots for a very smart pair that ended just above her ankles.

There was a cape with which to cover herself if it was raining, and she took that with her as a precaution.

Now at last she was ready.

She looked round the room to see if there was anything else she ought to pack.

Then she saw lying on a table in the window was her paint-box.

For a moment she hesitated, then she told herself it was something she might want.

The teachers at her School had told her she was talented at drawing and painting.

She had thought therefore that it would be a good idea for her to clean and restore some of the pictures that hung in the Manor.

Her mother had been very interested in them, but her father was indifferent.

Denise, Thelma remembered, had hardly glanced at them once she knew it was impossible for her to sell them.

Thelma had been very careful with those that were ancient and which had been handed down through the generations.

She cleaned away the dust of ages and restored them as her teachers had taught her to do.

Now she was leaving everything she loved including the pictures.

Her brother Ivan had been so proud of the house and everything it contained.

Thelma was five years younger than he was. Yet when they had played together as children it had usually been she who had thought of the mischief which made their laughter ring through the corridors.

It had echoed through the low rooms with their Elizabethan panelling.

It rung in the huge mediaeval Hall with the Fern coat-of-arms in stained glass.

When it was cold she would crouch in front of the fireplace where the whole trunk of a tree would be burned.

Thelma never felt she was alone there.

Her ancestors had assembled in the great Hall before a battle, to celebrate their weddings, and to mourn the dead.

She could feel them still watching and protecting her.

Now, she thought, she was running away from her

ancestors as well as the house where she had lived all her life.

Leaving her mother whose presence she could still feel in every room, especially her bed-room where she habitually sat.

"It is no use, Mama," she said in her heart, "I have to go! Otherwise I shall find myself married to Sir Richard because Stepmother will have the Law on her side, and Papa will never oppose her."

While she was thinking, she was packing her money.

Some in the pannier, some in the inside pocket of her riding-jacket.

It was then she thought of something else and it was important.

She ran downstairs, taking the precaution as she left her bed-room of locking the door.

She went to the Gun-room which opened off the hall.

It was a small room where her father kept his shooting-rifles.

The guns with which he shot game, and the rifle he used when he was stalking in Scotland.

Thelma knew he had several duelling-pistols in a drawer, two of them were smaller than the others and these she took out.

She inspected them to see if they were in working order. Finding nothing wrong she looked for the bullets that fitted them.

She found them in a small packet and put them into her pocket. She hid the pistols under her coat and went back upstairs.

Now at last she was ready.

Carrying the things she had packed, she walked along the corridor.

Down a side staircase which would take her to an exit nearer to the stables than any other.

She stepped out into the sunshine and just for a moment she felt panic-stricken.

She wondered, if she made a last desperate appeal to her father whether he would support her.

She knew however that even if he agreed to do so now, it was useless.

When evening came he would be drinking deeply of the rich claret and fiery brandy and he would be too drunk to argue with her Stepmother.

By that time the Chapel would be ready and it would be merely a case of sending for her father's Chaplain.

Thelma could see all too clearly the smirk there would be on Sir Richard's face when he returned with the Special Licence.

He thought of himself as a handsome man, but his eyes were too close together and his mouth was small and mean.

She was quite certain that he had no genuine feeling or affection for her Stepmother.

He admired her, and that was understandable.

Yet if she had not been able to entertain him in London with her husband's money, he would have ignored her.

As it was, Thelma thought, he rode her father's horses, and drank his wine.

If it became unavailable he would soon find somebody else to sponge on.

She was quite certain he would be only too pleased to marry anybody as rich as she was.

It would not only be a case of sharing her wealth with her Stepmother, which was what she intended, it would be with any other pretty woman who took Sir Richard's fancy.

It would not matter to him whether she was part of the *Beau Ton* or one of the disreputable creatures known as 'Cyprians'.

"How could I spend the rest of my life with a man like that?" she asked herself, and ran towards the stables.

She walked over the cobbled yard to where a stable-boy was standing. He touched his cap.

"Where is Watkins?" she asked.

" 'E be groomin' *Juno*, Miss Thelma."

She walked into the stables and found Watkins in the second stall.

*Juno* was a magnificent bay mare for which she knew he had a deep affection.

He took the greatest care of all the horses, but *Juno* was his favourite.

" 'Marnin', Miss Thelma!" Watkins said as she reached him.

He looked in surprise at what she was carrying.

Watkins was a small, wiry little man who had been her brother Ivan's Batman from the moment he had joined his Regiment.

After Ivan's death, Watkins, who had been slightly wounded, had been sent back to England.

He had called at once at the Manor to tell Lord Fernhurst how his son had met his death.

Thelma had listened to his tale. She knew as she did so how genuinely upset Watkins was and how much he had loved Ivan.

Her father had taken him on as one of his chief grooms, and Watkins had proved invaluable.

He was devoted to the horses, but he was also prepared to do anything else that was required of him.

He had transferred his love for Ivan to his sister.

Thelma knew now that she was going away that it was Watkins who must come with her.

Speaking little above a whisper, although there was no-one to overhear except the horses, she told him exactly what she had overheard.

Watkins listened in silence until she had finished her story.

"That be wrong, real wrong, Miss Thelma!" he exclaimed.

"How can I marry a man like that?"

" 'E be a bad'un, an' no rider either!"

"Then you will understand that I have to leave immediately!" Thelma said. "And I want you to come with me. I have plenty of money, and I thought you would carry some of it for safety."

She held out the bags of sovereigns and half-sovereigns.

Without arguing, Watkins put them away in his coat-pocket.

Then Thelma handed him one of the pistols and some bullets.

He took them too, and, as if they were just going for a ride in the Park, he asked:

"Well, now, which 'orse will ye be ridin', Miss Thelma?"

She hesitated a little, then said:

"If you come with me on *Juno*, I will take *Dragonfly*."

*Dragonfly* was the latest acquisition of her father's.

He had bought him the last time he was in London.

He was a magnificent stallion, and Lord Fernhurst had paid a large sum of money for him at Tattersall's.

He had had to outbid a number of other horse-owners.

Watkins did not argue about Thelma's choice, and there was a faint smile at the corners of his mouth as he went in to *Dragonfly*'s stall to saddle him.

He then saddled *Juno* before he took *Dragonfly* into the yard.

Thelma climbed onto the mounting-block and settled herself in the saddle.

Because *Dragonfly* was being a little obstreperous she moved ahead.

She left the stables by the back entrance which meant that no-one from the house would notice her departure or see in what direction she went.

27

It took Watkins just a few minutes to collect his own things and to put the saddle-bags on *Juno*'s back.

Then he caught up with Thelma.

As he did so, without speaking she moved quickly through the paddock and out into the meadowland beyond.

She was not quite certain where they were going, but instinctively she turned South.

The horses sprang forward and she told herself that this was the most thrilling, but also the most frightening thing she had ever done.

It was an adventure.

She was setting off into the unknown.

She had no idea what she would find, or how dangerous it might be.

# Chapter Two

They rode for some time in silence.

Thelma was thinking of what she had brought with her and wondering if she had left anything of importance behind.

She had not forgotten the letter from the Solicitors and she had slit it open when she began to change her clothes.

She had seen that it was a long one covering several pages, and would take time to read.

Time was the one thing she had not got. She had to be a long way from home when Sir Richard returned from Canterbury.

She therefore put the Solicitor's letter with her clothes and added to it several sheets of crested writing paper and some envelopes.

She knew she had to consider very carefully what she should reply.

She was terribly afraid that in some crafty manner her Stepmother would gain control of her money.

This made her think she would be wise to tell her father she had gone away, but time was passing and she was in a hurry to leave.

She therefore had put another piece of writing paper on her blotter and wrote:

*"Dearest Papa,*
*I am going away for a few days to stay with a friend. As*

*I have no wish to argue about it, I have not told Step-mother, but only you, that I am leaving.*

*I shall be thinking about you and hope you will be feeling better by the time I return.*

*My dearest love,*
*Your affectionate daughter,*
*Thelma."*

She put the letter in an envelope and left it on a table which stood outside her bed-room.

She knew her father's valet or the housemaid who looked after her would take it to him when he was awake.

Riding now beside Watkins into the unknown, she hoped she had thought of everything.

There would be a commotion when her Stepmother found she had disappeared.

Ordinarily Denise Fernhurst would have been glad to be rid of her.

But to-day when Sir Richard came back triumphantly bringing the Special Licence, there would be no bride.

As even to think of it made her afraid, Thelma rode a little quicker.

In two hours time they were a good number of miles from the Manor. Thelma was beginning to feel hungry and suspected that Watkins felt the same.

"Where shall we stop for luncheon?" she asked.

"There's a village not far from 'ere, Miss Thelma," he replied, "an' they'll 'ave bread and cheese if that'll do.'

"I am prepared to eat anything as long as I am not too long about it," Thelma smiled.

A mile or so further on they came to a picturesque black-and-white Inn standing at the side of a village green called "The Dog and Duck".

As there was a pond nearby with several ducks on it, Thelma thought it was aptly named.

They rode into the yard at the back of the Inn where as

they had expected there were stables.

Thelma dismounted, and Watkins took *Dragonfly*'s bridle from her. As he did so he said:

"I thinks, Miss Thelma, it'd be best if ye sat outside in th' sun or they'll be askin' a lot o' questions."

Thelma knew this was sound advice.

She therefore sat on a wooden bench which looked onto the green and had a table in front of it.

She imagined that in the evening it was where the villagers sat and drank after their day's work was over. Now there was nobody there except herself.

Watkins brought out her luncheon which was a small cottage loaf of freshly baked bread, a pat of butter and a large cheese.

She could dig into it with a spoon for the amount she wanted.

A jar of pickles came with it. Watkins explained that they were made by the Inn-keeper's wife.

Because she was hungry, Thelma found the fresh bread and cheese delicious.

When she and Watkins set off again she found it had cost only a few pence.

They had ridden for quite a way before Watkins said:

"I've bin thinkin', Miss Thelma, that if ye're 'idin', ye should change yer name."

Thelma looked at him in surprise before she said:

"Of course! You are right! It is something I should have thought of myself!"

"I did not think o' it 'til the Inn-keeper asked me who ye were,' Watkins went on.

"What did you tell him?' Thelma enquired.

"I said as 'ow I was takin' ye in a 'urry to join yer 'usband as 'as bin took ill."

Thelma's eyes widened, then she laughed.

"Whatever made you say that?"

"It wouldn't seem right," Watkins explained slowly, "for

a young Lady o' Quality to be travellin' about th' country-side with no-one t' look after 'er but a groom!"

Thelma thought this over and knew that Watkins was speaking sensibly.

Of course as a young girl she should have a chaperon.

She was so used to riding about her father's Estate alone that she had not realised that in the world outside people would think it strange.

"It was very quick of you to think of an answer like that," she said, "and I think it is something we might stick to in the future. Now – what shall I call myself – ?"

She thought as she spoke it must obviously not be too close to her own name. Anyway it was an amusing idea to change her identity.

They were riding across-country and avoiding the roads.

It came to her mind that she might be 'Mrs. Field', 'Mrs. Meadows', or 'Mrs. Wood.'

They all sounded rather dull and she was sure she could think of something more exciting.

Then they came to a stream, having pulled in their horses, and Watkins said:

"It be quite shallow, Miss, an' I thinks we can ford it."

Thelma gave an exclamation.

"That is what I will call myself – 'Mrs. Forde' with an 'E'!"

Watkins grinned and she went on:

"That is exactly what we are doing, Watkins! Crossing a ford from one world into another."

She thought that Watkins would not follow what she was saying, but he remarked:

"That's wot I'll call ye, Miss Thelma, from now on – 'Mrs. Forde', an' we're on our way to where yer 'usband be a waitin' for ye."

Thelma laughed.

"Having forded the stream, we are riding on towards the distant hills," she said.

32

Because she did not want to overtire the horses they stopped late in the afternoon at another Inn.

It was in an isolated part of the country.

Thelma was sure that even if they were surprised at her appearance and talked about it, there would be no-one to listen.

The Inn seemed quiet and small and at first she was half-afraid it could not accommodate them.

She sent Watkins to enquire if they could stay the night.

When he came back he reported that the place seemed clean and the stables adequate, and the Inn-keeper's wife had hurried upstairs to put clean sheets on the beds.

Thelma therefore helped Watkins put the horses in the stables.

After being unsaddled they had a good meal which they had brought with them.

Thelma knew as she groomed *Dragonfly* that it was an inexpressible comfort to have with her a horse she loved.

Then she went into the Inn.

It was very small with low beamed ceilings, and the only occupant of the Bar was a very old man who was practically blind.

The Inn-keeper was obviously overcome with her appearance.

" 'Tis a great honour, M'Lady," he said, "ter 'ave ye wi' us. Oi only 'opes we can make ye comfortable."

"I am sure I shall be," Thelma smiled, "but I confess to feeling very hungry."

She went up the narrow, rickety stairs to find her bedroom. It was very sparsely furnished.

But it was clean, and she saw there was a goose-feather mattress which she knew would be comfortable.

She took off her riding-hat and jacket to wash in cold water.

Watkins had arranged with the Inn-keeper for them to use the Private Parlour which was again very small and,

Thelma suspected, seldom used.

She ate a simple meal without being watched by strangers, and she was glad not to have to talk to anybody.

When she had finished she opened the letter which had come from her Great-Aunt's Solicitors.

She had also brought downstairs with her the writing paper and envelopes she had taken from the Manor.

She had been thinking while she was riding that she must make sure that her money was intact when she came to claim it.

She was not quite certain how to do so.

The letter from the Solicitors was quite straightforward.

They had written to inform her father that they had the honour of acting for the late Dowager Duchess of Winterton and they enclosed a copy of her Will.

As Thelma read the next three pages her eyes widened as she realised she was now not rich, but very rich indeed!

Her Great-Aunt had left her monies amounting to nearly a million pounds.

Also jewellery, pictures and furniture that were at present in the house in which she had lived on the Duke's estate in Huntingdonshire.

There followed an Inventory of the most important items.

All of which Thelma knew she was thrilled to own and which she would always treasure.

The letter finished with a request for her father, as her Guardian, to give the Firm his instructions as soon as possible.

Because it was all so unexpected and overwhelming, Thelma read the letter through a second time.

Then after some deliberation she made up her mind.

She asked the Inn-keeper's wife if she could have a bottle of ink and a pen.

This took some time before it was forthcoming, and

34

when it was on the table in front of her Thelma wrote carefully:

*"To: Messrs. Marlow, Thestlethwaite and Downing."*

She thanked them for their letter and continued:

*"My daughter Thelma, who is heir to all the monies and the items you have described to me as being in my Aunt's Will, is now away from home."*

*I, myself, am in ill-health and cannot receive you. I therefore instruct you on behalf of my daughter to continue to administer the funds as you have done hitherto, and to keep the other properties safely until such time as my daughter is in touch with you.*

*On no account should anyone else have access to anything which belongs to her, or to make any decisions or requests on her behalf.*

*Only when she comes to see you personally, which she will do as soon as it is possible, can her own decisions about her new acquisitions be made.*

*As her father and Guardian, I hereby permit her to make up her own mind on any questions appertaining to her new property without interference from any other persons.*

> *Yours truly,*
> *Fernhurst."*

Thelma signed her father's name as she had done in the past.

She did it so skilfully that she knew it would be impossible for anyone to contend that it had not been signed by him.

In his present state she suspected he would not be able to remember whether he had signed it or not.

She put the letter into an envelope and addressed it to the Solicitors. Before she went up to bed she asked the Inn-keeper to make sure it was posted the following morning.

He assured her that it would be.

She expected to lie awake worrying about herself and her future, but the goose-feather mattress was so comfortable that she fell asleep almost at once.

Thelma awoke to the sound of a cockerel crowing outside.

She could hear the Inn-keeper and his wife stirring below.

After a large breakfast of bacon and ham she helped Watkins to saddle the horses, and they set off once again.

When they were away from the village Watkins asked:

" 'Ave ye any idea, Miss Thelma, where we be agoin'?"

"None at all!" Thelma answered. "I thought the first step was to get as far away from the Manor as quickly as we could just in case Her Ladyship or Sir Richard searched for us.'

"We'd best be careful they don't find us," Watkins said laconically.

Thelma was quite certain that he disliked her Step-mother, as did the other servants.

She knew they had been happy at the Manor when they had adored her mother.

She thought she would never forget their white, tearful faces at her mother's Funeral or the way in which for a long time when they spoke about her it was in choked voices.

She knew too that they were shocked at the way her Stepmother was behaving with Sir Richard Leith.

At the same time, Thelma was sensible enough to realise that she could not stay away from home for ever.

After writing the letter last night she thought perhaps in several month's time she might find an older member of her

36

family – preferably a man – who would support her against her Stepmother.

Perhaps her father would miss her when she did not come back and would make some effort to 'pull himself together'.

It was all rather vague, and it was impossible to make plans too far ahead.

All she was acutely aware of was that her Stepmother would try by every means in her power to get hold of her money.

If she was at home, she would certainly be forced into marriage with Sir Richard.

If she refused Denise would try other ways of gaining control of a million pounds.

It was frightening to think about.

"She might even end by murdering me!" Thelma told herself.

She shivered, knowing it was an actual possibility.

'The only thing I can be certain of,' she went on in her mind, 'is that I must stay away from home until I can find some means of revealing where I am without being intimidated.'

For the moment that seemed impossible.

She therefore tried to concentrate on where she should go.

She reckoned that by this time they were nearing the coast and might be, she thought, in East Sussex.

She wished she had a map, but that was something she had not thought of bringing with her.

They therefore rode on.

At luncheontime Watkins once again found a wayside Inn, but this one was not as pleasant as those they had encountered before.

There were a number of men in the Bar who peered through the windows at Thelma.

They made comments that she could not hear, but which

evoked roars of laughter.

Once again she had bread and cheese.

But the cottage loaf was stale, the butter rancid; while the cheese was inferior.

They moved on as quickly as they could and Watkins was angry, not only about the food but the dirt in the stables.

"We'll be more careful, Miss Thelma, where us goes 'nother time."

Thelma agreed with him.

All the same she was afraid of going to the better-class Posting Inns on the main roads.

She knew her appearance would cause a great deal of comment, as would the superiority of their horses.

She knew too that should somebody notice her they might inadvertently be the cause of her Stepmother's learning where she was.

Then she would be lost.

'But I cannot go on like this for ever!' she felt despairingly.

As they passed through a wood in the shadow of the trees as a relief from the heat of the sun, she saw on the other side of the ride a magnificent-looking house.

In fact with a wood behind it it looked like a jewel in a velvet setting.

Thelma drew in her horse to stare at it and Watkins did the same.

"I wonder who lives there?" she asked.

He did not answer and after a moment Thelma said:

"Let us go and look at it more closely. It is the sort of mansion I have always wanted to see."

She remembered how the girls at School had boasted of the houses and Castles in which their parents lived.

On one occasion she had stayed at Warwick Castle which had thrilled and delighted her.

The history of it, the grey stone towers and the rooms in which Kings and Queens had been entertained, was breathtaking.

Another time a friend had taken her to Longleat, where the Thynne family had lived for generations.

To Thelma it was the Fairy Palace of her dreams and she had thought about it so often and wished she could go there again.

Now she was determined to see the house that lay ahead of her.

She and Watkins rode down into the valley where there was a small village.

The cottages were thatched, their gardens bright with spring flowers.

At the end of the village she saw what she knew was the entrance to the owner's house.

Large wrought-iron gates, tipped with gold, had on either side identical stone lodges.

The gates were open and without really meaning to, Thelma rode through them.

As she expected there was a long drive flanked by ancient oak trees. Watkins glanced at her as if he was asking a question.

"I just want to look a little closer," Thelma said. "If anybody challenges us we can ask them who lives here, and say we have inadvertently come to the wrong house."

She laughed and Watkins grinned as they rode on.

When they were still some distance from the house, Thelma gave an exclamation.

Immediately to their left, which they had not noticed before because of the trees, there was a huge tent.

There was also a number of strange-looking vehicles standing around it, which looked as if they could house animals.

"It is a Circus!" she exclaimed. "How exciting!"

For the moment she forgot the house and rode towards the tent.

It was a large one and before she reached it, she saw coming from the opening a man holding a tiger on a lead.

It was so surprising and so unexpected that Thelma drew

in *Dragonfly* and stopped to watch.

It was a large and, she thought, a fairly old tiger.

The man took it to one of the vehicles which she could now see was a cage.

The tiger sprang into it without any persuasion and the man, having taken off its lead, shut the door and bolted it.

Because she was so intrigued, Thelma moved a little closer.

Now she could see there were six cages containing lions, leopards, cheetahs and half-a-dozen monkeys.

She was so interested that she dismounted from *Dragonfly* and as Watkins took her bridle she walked first to the lions' cage.

They were two magnificent beasts.

From the look of them she thought they were well-fed and in excellent health.

She stood there for some minutes and was just going to move to another cage when she heard a sound inside the Big Top.

Because she was curious she walked in.

It was exactly as she expected, with seats rising all round it for the spectators to sit on.

In the Ring a young horse was bucking and rearing.

A man, who was obviously a groom or perhaps a performer, was holding him by the bridle, while another man was watching, obviously amused at the contest.

With a final buck the horse won.

He pulled the reins out of the groom's hand and still bucking galloped out of the back of the tent.

The groom ran after him while the other man laughed a spontaneous sound which made Thelma laugh too.

It was then that the man in the centre of the tent saw her.

For a moment he just stared at her, then he walked in her direction.

As he did so she was aware that he was a Gentleman.

He was also extremely handsome, tall with broad shoulders, and she thought about thirty years of age.

He was not wearing a hat and his dark hair was swept back from a square forehead.

He was wearing riding-breeches with only a shirt and a cravat round his neck which was tied carelessly, as if he was obviously not particularly interested in his appearance.

When he reached her he said:

"Good-afternoon! If you have come to see a performance, I am afraid you are too early! It does not take place until to-morrow."

"I was, as it happens, just curious," Thelma replied, "when I saw a tiger being led from the tent."

The Gentleman smiled.

"I can understand that you found it somewhat unexpected in the English countryside!"

"Just as I find lions and monkeys unusual," Thelma smiled.

"Then of course I must introduce you to my Circus," the Gentleman said.

"*Your* Circus? Then you own it?"

"I own the animals which have come from my menagerie."

Thelma gave a little gasp.

"How exciting! I have always wanted to see a menagerie! For of course I have heard of them."

"Then I could not be so ungracious as not to show it to you,' the Gentleman said. "At the same time, as they are performing in the Circus they will not appear at their best."

"Why not?" Thelma enquired.

"Because they are accustomed to the quiet and privacy of their own quarters. Now they have to show off in public."

There was a hard note in the Gentleman's voice, which made Thelma look at him in surprise.

They had walked together while he was speaking outside the tent. Now they stopped, as Thelma had done before, in front of the lions.

"I brought Sambo back with me from India," the Gentleman said. "He was then just a tiny cub, and Sita was given to me three years ago, and it will break my heart to part with them!"

"To part with them?" Thelma ejaculated.

The Gentleman did not answer.

He was undoing the cage of the lions.

Sambo, who Thelma was sure was a magnificent specimen, moved towards him and rubbed his head against his arm.

As if Sita was not to be outdone, she tried to catch the Gentleman's attention by rubbing her nose against his shirt.

"You can see they love me!" the Gentleman said to Thelma almost defiantly.

"They do indeed!" she answered. "That is why I cannot understand why you should part with them."

Again the Gentleman did not reply.

Instead he patted the lions and moved from the cage to shut and bolt the door as they watched him through the bars.

He looked at them for a long moment before he said:

"I must not encroach on your time, Madam, and if you would like to attend the performance here to-morrow, then of course I will keep a seat for you."

He appeared to draw in his breath as he said:

"It will cost you the sum of one sovereign!"

Thelma looked at him in astonishment.

She knew it was an enormous sum of money for a ticket to a Circus.

Although she had never attended one, the Circus which occasionally came to the Market Town nearest to the

Manor charged only one shilling for the best seats.

The Gentleman was obviously waiting for her to leave and after a moment's silence she said:

"I wonder if you would be so kind as to advise me where I and my groom can stay for the night? We have been travelling all day, and have still a long way to go to-morrow."

"You are travelling alone with your groom?" the Gentleman asked.

There was enough surprise in his voice to tell Thelma that Watkins had been right.

She must have a good explanation for what she was doing.

"My name," she said quickly, "is Mrs. Forde. My husband has been taken ill, and I am therefore trying to reach him by the quickest route."

"I understand," the Gentleman said, "and of course I should be honoured if you would be my guest."

"You mean . . stay here?' Thelma asked.

He waved his hand in the direction of the house on the other side of the lake.

"I am the Earl of Merstone."

"I think it is the most beautiful house I have ever seen!" Thelma exclaimed.

"That is what I have always thought myself," the Earl replied, "and although I am afraid you will not be very comfortable, I hope you will nevertheless not refuse to be my guest."

"I shall be delighted, if you are certain it will not inconvenience you?' Thelma said.

He smiled as if she had said something absurd. Then he called to the man she had seen leading the tiger saying:

"Bring me *Mercury*, Dan!"

"Very good, M'Lord."

The man ran to the back of the tent.

As Thelma stood waiting she was aware that the Earl was

looking at the house glowing in the evening sunshine.

There was an expression on his face which she did not understand.

Dan came back leading a horse that was a nice-looking animal, but by no means the equal of *Dragonfly* or *Juno*.

The Earl did not comment however as he helped Thelma into the saddle of *Dragonfly*.

Yet she knew by his expression that he appreciated how outstanding the stallion was.

They rode away from the Circus and crossed an ancient stone bridge which spanned the lake and went up towards the great house.

The nearer she came to it the more magnificent Thelma realised it was.

The sun was shining on the windows and the stone urns and statues on the roof were silhouetted against the blue of the sky.

It looked, she thought, as if it came straight out of a Fairy Story.

When they reached the front-door the Earl dismounted and lifted Thelma to the ground.

As she felt his hands round her waist she told herself that he was very strong.

He was also very attractive, in fact more attractive than any man she had seen before.

As he set her down the Earl said to Watkins:

"If you will follow me, I will show you the way to the stables, but you will have to groom your own horses."

"That's all right, M'Lord, I be used to it," Watkins replied.

Thelma thought with a little smile that Watkins had found out who was the owner of the house.

She had seen him talking to one of the boys working round the tents, and she was certain he would gain any information he could.

"Go inside," the Earl said to Thelma, "I shall not be long."

She walked up the long flight of stone steps.

The front-door was open and she went into a large, very impressive Hall.

There was a carved and gilded staircase on one side and a huge stone mantelpiece stretched half-way up the wall on the other.

For a moment she found herself entranced by the beautiful way in which it was designed.

The sunlight came through high windows to illuminate the pictures that hung on the walls.

Then she was aware, and it was quite a shock, that the walls were in need of repair.

The wooden floor was unpolished, and the ashes from a long dead fire still remained in the grate.

She looked a little closer.

The stair-carpet was threadbare and the long curtains hanging on either side of the windows were faded.

She could see that the lining of one of them was torn away and was hanging down untidily.

She looked round her in bewilderment.

How was it possible that such a magnificent house could be in such a state?

There was no sign of the Earl.

After what he had said to Watkins, she had the idea there were no grooms in the stables.

There certainly seemed to be no servants in the house and she walked across the Hall to open a door at the end of it.

It was, as she expected, a Salon and there were three great chandeliers hanging from the ceiling.

Their tapers were half-burnt, their wax had spilled over the crystal.

The room itself was beautifully proportioned. But the

Louis XIV furniture with its gilded arms and legs needed recovering.

There were marks on the walls where pictures or perhaps mirrors had once hung, and the Sèvres china that stood on the mantelpiece needed washing.

She stood looking at it.

She was thinking it was a crime to let anything so perfect become so dirty when the Earl came into the room.

As he saw her look round he said in a voice that was harsh and bitter:

"Perhaps now that you have seen the inside of my house you would prefer to go elsewhere?"

"No . . no . . of course . . not," Thelma replied. "At the same time, please tell me what has . . happened here. How has it . . come to this . . state?"

There was a twist to the Earl's lips as he said:

"Surely you are not so foolish as to need to be told the obvious?"

Thelma did not speak and he went on:

"The explanation is quite simple: I cannot afford servants, I cannot afford to live here, and I cannot afford to keep my menagerie!"

Thelma stared at him.

"I . . I am sorry," she murmured.

As if the softness of her voice infuriated him he said angrily:

"I do not need your pity! If it is not good enough for you, then you can just get out and go somewhere else!"

His voice seemed to echo round the room.

Because the way he spoke frightened her Thelma took a step backwards.

# Chapter Three

Instinctively, because her heart was beating so tumul-
tuously, Thelma put her hand up to her breast.

Then as the Earl looked at her the expression on his face
altered.

'Forgive me,' he said, "I did not mean to frighten you."

She did not answer, and he went on:

"It is inexcusable, but perhaps you will be generous
enough to try and understand."

"I . . I would like to," Thelma said in a hesitating little
voice, "but . . I did not . . intend to . . make you angry."

"I promise I am very apologetic," the Earl said. "Please
sit down, and I will try to explain."

Because she felt as if her legs could not carry her, Thelma
sat down on the nearest sofa.

The Earl stood in front of the mantelpiece.

Thelma was aware that, as in the Hall, the ashes from the
fire had not been cleared, and the fire-irons were unpolished.

"When I came back from France a month ago," the Earl
said, "I found my home in this chaos."

"You were in France?" Thelma interrupted.

"With the Army. I fought against Napoleon for six years,
then after Waterloo the Duke of Wellington insisted I
stayed with him in the Army of Occupation."

Thelma was listening. She was thinking as she did so that
so many people had suffered owing to the war.

47

"I left my cousin in charge of the house," the Earl continued. "He is older than I am, and I thought I could trust him."

"But . . he betrayed . . you?"

"He betrayed me, and instead of looking after everything until I got back, he left the place as you now see it!"

"How could he . . do such a thing?" Thelma asked.

"I suppose it was naive of me not to realise that he was jealous because I hold the position that he wants for himself!"

"But . . surely . . it is not as bad as it . . seems?"

"It is worse," the Earl said, "far, far worse! I not only have the house crumbling about my ears, but the pensioners, the farmers, and of course the animals!"

The Earl's voice softened as he spoke of his menagerie.

Thelma, clasping her hands together, said:

"When I looked at them I thought how well they seemed and felt sure they had been properly fed."

The bitterness in the Earl's voice intensified as he replied:

"Two people remained loyal to me – the men I had left in charge of my menagerie. When there was no money left they killed off the deer in the Park."

He drew in a deep breath before he said:

"And now they are finished."

"So that is why you are holding a Circus."

"It is a last desperate attempt," he said, "to save my animals. Otherwise they will have to be destroyed."

Thelma gave a little cry.

"Oh, no! That must not happen!"

"It all depends on how much I take at my unusual and the most expensive Circus that has ever been."

He sat down in a chair near her before he said:

"It is a wild gamble, but however much money I get it is not likely to last for long."

There was a note of despair in his voice which told

Thelma without words how much his animals meant to him.

A little nervously, because she was frightened he might be angry she asked tentatively:

"Is there . . nothing in . . the house that . . you could . . sell?"

"Do you suppose I have not thought of that?" the Earl enquired. "As you might have guessed, the house and its contents are entailed at the moment onto my cousin."

"You mean . . he is your Heir Presumptive?"

"Exactly, and he is of course banking on the fact that I cannot afford to marry and have a son."

"It is frightening . . very frightening," Thelma said, "but I feel sure there is . . something you . . can do."

"Then tell me what that is, and I will do it."

As if she had once again upset him the Earl rose to his feet.

"Now that you have seen the inside of what was once a great house," he said, "I think it would be wise to be on your way."

Thelma looked at him in consternation.

She realised it was growing late, she was tired, and she was sure the horses were too.

"You . . you did invite . . me to . . stay," she faltered.

"In this mess?" the Earl asked. "My dear Lady, I can see from your appearance that you are accustomed to something very much better than I can possibly provide here!"

Thelma did not answer.

She got up from the sofa and walked across the room to the window.

Outside there was what had once been a beautiful rose-garden, but now it was a mass of weeds. Yet she knew that in a month the roses would be in bloom.

The lilac trees were in bud and the first blossoms of syringa were opening out beside them.

It was wild and untidy, but it was beautiful.

Something within her responded to its beauty in a way

she did not understand.

Behind her she heard the Earl rise from his chair and walk towards her.

She did not look up when he reached her. She only said in a very small voice:

"Please . . let me stay . . I have . . nowhere else . . to go."

He looked at her in surprise for a moment, then he asked:

"What do you mean – you have nowhere to go?"

Thelma realised she had spoken without thinking and looked up at him, her eyes dark and worried.

"The horses are . . tired," she stammered. "I have . . ridden a long way."

"Then of course you must stay," the Earl said. "Come, I will show you where you can sleep."

He walked from the Salon and outside into the Hall where Watkins was waiting.

He was holding the panniers which contained Thelma's clothes and also the bag which had been fixed to her saddle.

"The horses are all right?" the Earl asked.

"They're comfortable, thank ye, M'Lord."

The Earl started to climb the stairs with Thelma beside him.

Watkins followed behind.

They reached a landing on which she guessed were the State Bed-rooms.

She knew she was not mistaken when the Earl opened the first door he came to.

The room was certainly magnificent with a huge four-poster bed, carved and gilded, but the furniture was covered with dust and the curtains needed repairing.

"This is the best I can offer you," the Earl said in a hard voice.

"It is beautiful!" Thelma said, "and I am very grateful."

The Earl turned to Watkins.

"You will find the linen-cupboard beyond the green baize door at the end of the passage. You will have to make up your mistress's bed. There is no one else to do it!"

'That's all right, M'Lord," Watkins replied. "I'll see to it!"

He put the saddle-bag and the panniers down on a chair and left the room.

Thelma looked around.

"The pictures are magnificent!" she said. "And so is the furniture."

"It is all entailed," the Earl said, "while I starve!"

He walked towards the door as he spoke. When he reached it he looked back to say:

"I imagine there is something for us to eat at dinner, but do not be too optimistic."

He shut the door sharply behind him.

Thelma gave a little sigh. She was sorry for him – desperately sorry.

At the same time, she was very grateful to have somewhere to stay.

In a way it was exciting to see inside one of the most beautiful houses she had ever imagined.

Watkins came back about ten minutes later, bringing sheets edged with lace.

"This be a nice 'how-de-do', an' no mistake, Miss Thelma," he remarked.

"It is certainly very surprising," Thelma agreed. "Are there any maid-servants in the house?"

"There's one old woman in th' kitchen," Watkins answered, "an' an old man, so crippled wi' arthritis 'e can 'ardly walk!"

"You will have to help them prepare the dinner."

"I guessed that," Watkins replied, "but at least we've got a roof over our 'eads, as we don't 'ave to pay for."

"We will pay for what we eat," Thelma said quickly. "His Lordship has no money and we cannot impose upon him."

"No money?" Watkins queried.

He deftly made the bed with an experienced hand and he asked Thelma if she would like some hot water.

When he disappeared she unpacked one of the gowns she had put in the pannier.

Because it was made of the most expensive gauze, when she shook it out the creases disappeared and she hung it up in the wardrobe.

When Watkins had brought her some hot water in a brass can that was almost black because it needed polishing, she started to undress.

Everything in the room was saleable.

She was knowledgeable enough to know that the pictures were by distinguished artists and very valuable.

It was not difficult to realise what a torture it must be for any man to be surrounded by such treasure, but at the same time to be completely penniless.

'I must help him,' she thought.

Then she was surprised at her own feelings.

Somehow, she thought, she must try to cheer up the Earl.

She took a great deal of trouble over arranging her hair and thought, when she had done so, that in her gauze gown she looked very elegant.

When she entered the Salon she found the Earl waiting for her in his evening-clothes.

He had looked handsome and striking before. In knee-breeches, black silk stockings and a cut-away coat he looked as magnificent as the house.

As she advanced towards him he smiled at her and said:

"As you were kind enough to be my guest, I have raided the cellar. I found to my surprise a bottle of champagne, which I feel will be more to your taste than claret."

"I would like a glass," Thelma answered. "At the same time, perhaps you ought to keep it for a more auspicious occasion."

"Now you are fishing for compliments," the Earl said, "and I assure you nothing could be more auspicious at the moment than, instead of sitting alone in misery, to be dining with a very beautiful Lady!"

Thelma bobbed him a curtsy.

"Thank you," she said, "I am sure I too will find it very auspicious!"

They both laughed.

The Earl opened the bottle of champagne and handed her a glass.

"I had no idea it was still there," he said. "I should certainly have drunk it before now to drown my sorrows!"

Thelma raised her glass.

"To your Circus to-morrow evening," she said, "and may it be a great success."

"To make sure of that," the Earl said, "I think you should take part in it!"

Thelma laughed.

"I doubt if anyone would look at me when they can see your marvellous animals!"

"I think the human element is also important," the Earl said, "and you and your horse would certainly get plenty of attention."

"Tell me exactly what you intend to do," Thelma begged. "Have you hired the tent and all the seats?"

She thought as she spoke that must be quite an expensive item.

The Earl shook his head.

"No, I was fortunate," he replied. "I learnt from my men that five years ago when the war was still raging, the Circus that used to come here every year folded."

"That was sad!" Thelma exclaimed.

She was thinking of the wandering Circus which had

come when she was a child to the nearest Market Town.

She had never been allowed to go to it, but the children in the village used to hang around the Big Top, and stare at the animals in their cages.

"I suppose," she added, "that a great number of enterprises like Circuses have suffered from the war, and can no longer keep going."

"Exactly," the Earl replied, "including my home, my farms and the people employed here!"

The bitterness was back in his voice.

"Go on telling me about the Circus," Thelma said hastily.

"The men from the Circus asked if they could leave the tents and the other equipment in one of my barns, fortunately without approaching my cousin, who would undoubtedly have said 'No'!"

He gave a twisted smile.

"It was when I saw all that equipment there that I thought of having a Circus, hoping to earn enough money to continue to keep my animals."

"And do you think people will come?"

Thelma asked the question a little nervously. She was afraid that once again she might upset the Earl.

"I have already notified my neighbours of what is taking place," he replied, "and I think a number of them realise the straits in which I find myself."

"You have not yet told me what your animals can do."

"The two men who kept the animals alive," he answered, "despite my cousin's dislike of them have taught them a few tricks.

"One of my tigers, whose name is Jacko, will jump through a hoop, the lions will chase each other round and round the ring. The monkeys will perform any antic which takes their fancy."

Thelma clapped her hands.

"It sounds entrancing, and what else do you have?"

"There are cheetahs, and I also have a giraffe which in itself looks peculiar to people who have not seen one before!"

Thelma laughed.

"That includes me! I would love to see a giraffe!"

At that moment Watkins appeared at the Drawing-Room to say:

"Dinner's served, M'Lord!"

Thelma thought the Earl looked surprised, and she explained:

"Watkins has been helping in the kitchen with the dinner, and actually he is quite a good cook."

"You are fortunate to have him!" the Earl remarked.

"Watkins was my brother's Batman," Thelma explained, "and when he was killed my father employed him as a groom."

The Earl did not reply and they walked down the passage.

As Thelma had expected, the Dining-Room, which was very large, was also very impressive.

There were huge portraits of previous Earls on the walls, and the big table in the centre of the room could hold thirty guests.

She tried not to look at the dust everywhere, including the tops of the pictures.

There was one candelabrum holding four candles.

It stood at the top of the table in front of a high-backed chair carved with the Earl's coat-of-arms.

She sat down next to him. She felt as if they were on a tiny island of light, while the rest of the world was in darkness.

Watkins brought in the food.

There was soup which was well flavoured and she knew he must have had a hand in it, and after that there was rabbit which was at least edible.

With it were a few very small Brussels sprouts and some potatoes.

The Earl ate as if he was hungry, and because Thelma was hungry too, she ate everything that was offered.

That however was the end of the meal.

She knew by the expression on Watkins' face and the look he gave her that he had done his best.

But as he would have said himself:

" 'Yer can't make bricks without straw!' "

The Earl picked up the bottle of champagne. When he had filled Thelma's glass she said:

"Please . . no more . . I am not used to drinking."

He raised his eye-brows but did not say anything.

Then, their small meal being over, he sat back in his chair and said:

"Now I suggest you tell me about yourself."

Thelma looked away from him.

"There is . . not much to tell."

"But, where are you going – and why?"

There was silence. Then he said:

"I think you should tell me the truth."

Again there was silence until Thelma said:

"I do not know why you should be curious."

The Earl laughed.

"You cannot really be as naive as that! Just think what has happened!"

"What has?"

"I am in the depths of despair trying to organise my Circus when out of the blue a very beautiful, smartly dressed Lady appears. She consents to become my guest."

He paused before he went on:

"She is travelling alone with a groom and tells me that unless she stays she has nowhere else to go."

Again the Earl paused before he asked:

"Would you not be curious if that happened to you?"

"I am Mrs. Forde – I am hurrying to my husband – who is ill – and it is – quicker to – travel across-country."

Thelma told the story jerkily as if she was trying to

56

remember what Watkins had said.

She disliked lying, and because that was what she was doing the colour rose in her face.

Unexpectedly the Earl put out his hand.

He smiled at her and said:

"Put your hand in mine."

Without thinking, she did as he told her.

For a moment his fingers closed over hers, then he looked down at the third finger of her left hand.

"No wedding-ring?" he asked quietly. "And I also suspect – no husband!"

Thelma snatched her hand from his.

"That is cheating," she exclaimed, "and you took me by surprise!"

She thought as she spoke it was very stupid of her not to have provided herself with a wedding-ring.

She had thought she had packed everything she needed.

But to adopt Watkins' story without making it plausible had been very foolish.

"Now, let me hear the truth," the Earl said. "You have run away!"

"As you think you are so clever," Thelma retorted, "you can just guess, but I shall not tell you whether you are right or wrong."

"Very well, then," the Earl said, "I shall guess."

He looked at her as she sat beside him.

Her hair was shining in the light of the candles, her eyes were a little wary, at the same time very beautiful.

He took in the elegance of her expensive gown, her slimness and immature figure.

He told himself she might have stepped down from one of the pictures hanging on the wall and was in fact not real, but a part of his imagination.

Because he was silent, she said after a minute or so:

"I am waiting."

"I am thinking a great many things," the Earl said, "but

as you wish to be secretive, I will not intrude."

Thelma laughed, and it was a very pretty sound.

"As this is a situation that is of your own making, be honest and admit that you do not know!'

"I can presume a great deal," the Earl replied, "but I would not wish to upset you by being wrong, or make you nervous by being right.'

Thelma laughed again.

"Now you are just being wily, so let me keep my secrets to myself."

"Very well," the Earl agreed, "but you must give me a name by which I can address you."

"It is Thelma," she answered.

"A very attractive name," he said, "for a very attractive person."

Because she thought it was a mistake to be serious, she said lightly:

"You sound sincere, but I am sure you have said that to a great many attractive women, and you thought it up first when you were in the bath!"

Now the Earl laughed, and it was a spontaneous sound.

Somehow as if it had 'broken the ice' they started to talk more freely.

The Earl told her about the fighting in the Peninsula, the defeat of Napoleon at Waterloo and some of the problems in the Army of Occupation.

She found it entrancing.

They sat on in the Dining-Room until the candles were beginning to gut low, and the Earl had nearly finished the bottle of champagne.

Thelma rose to her feet.

"I think I should go to bed," she said, "and I am sure you will want to rise early to-morrow morning, as there will be a lot to do before the performance in the evening."

"A very great deal," the Earl agreed, "and you are going to stay and help me!"

It was a statement rather than a question.

"Do you really want me?" Thelma asked.

"Of course I want you," he said. "If you leave me now, I shall be convinced that you have never existed and I merely imagined you!"

They walked slowly from the Dining-Room towards the Salon in silence.

As the Earl opened the door she could see that somebody, and she suspected it was Watkins, had lit one of the chandeliers and also the candles on the mantelpiece.

The room looked lovely.

In the soft light from the candles the dust was hardly visible.

She went towards the fireplace.

Instead of the old ashes, there was a small wood fire burning there.

She turned to the Earl to say:

"It seems very cosy at night!"

He was nearer to her than she had suspected, and was looking at her in a strange way.

Then before she could speak again he said:

"You are lovely! Far too lovely to be wandering about alone without somebody to protect you."

"I have Watkins."

"I was not thinking of servants."

She did not understand, and after a moment he went on:

"A month ago I would have known the answer to that, but now I can only offer you a place in my house, if you can ignore the discomfort of it."

"There is no reason for you to talk like that," Thelma replied, "and if you will forgive me for saying so, I think you are being unnecessarily despondent."

"Why?" the Earl enquired.

"Because I am sure there is something you can do about your position."

"Actually," he corrected, "I was talking about yours."

There was a faint smile on his lips and an expression in his eyes that Thelma did not see.

"I am thinking of your position," Thelma said in a serious little voice. "I am sure if you went through the Inventory, and it must be a large one for such a big house, you might find something – a picture, an ornament, or perhaps a piece of furniture – which is not entailed and could be sold."

The Earl looked at her in a different way from what he had done before.

"Perhaps you are right," he said after a moment, "but when I returned here I was so appalled at what I found that all I could think about was my animals!"

"I can understand that," Thelma said, "but I would like, with your permission, to check over the pictures, not those in the grand rooms like this, or the Picture Gallery, if you have one, but in places where they might have been forgotten or overlooked."

The Earl spread out his hands in an eloquent gesture.

" 'Everything I have is yours', as they say in the East. Now you are giving me hope."

"That is what I want you to have," Thelma replied. "How could anybody live in this magnificent house, especially a soldier, and accept defeat?"

"You are challenging me!"

"That is what I want to do, and I would like to see you being much more courageous and optimistic than you appear at the moment!"

She looked at him provocatively as she spoke.

At the same time she was a little afraid he might be offended.

Instead he said:

"I was talking about you."

"You told me I could remain a mystery," Thelma said quickly, "and that is what I want to be."

"A mystery is meant to be unravelled."

"There will be time for that later," Thelma replied. "Now we have to concentrate on you and the most important thing is, as you so rightly said, to feed the animals."

She put out her hand and started counting on her fingers:

"The second is to clean the house, and for that you need servants. The third, to look after your tenant-farmers who, like those in other parts of the country, having suffered from the war are now suffering in the peace, and lastly . . . '

As she spoke she held up her little finger.

"Yes – lastly?" the Earl asked.

"To make you happy."

She spoke quite innocently.

She was thinking as she did so that it was wrong that anyone so handsome and so outstanding in personality should be in the depths of despair.

She knew from the way the Earl talked and the expression on his face that he was still suffering from the shock.

First from finding his house in such a state, and secondly from what could only be the horror of discovering he was without money.

"If you want me to be happy," the Earl said quietly, "there is quite an obvious answer to that."

Thelma looked up at him.

There was an expression in his eyes she had not seen there before, and she felt vibrations from him that were unexpected.

She was suddenly conscious that everything had altered.

She was not quite certain how or in what way. She only knew that something about the Earl made her feel shy.

"Now, as I have said before," she said quickly, "it is getting late, and I am tired."

She put out her hand as she spoke adding:

"Thank you very much for having me to stay, and for being so very kind."

The Earl took her hand in both of his.

"You are tired," he said, "and therefore I must let you go to bed and – sleep."

There was a distinct pause before the last word.

"At what time do you have breakfast?" Thelma asked.

She took her hand from his as she spoke, and was aware as she did so that he seemed reluctant to let it go.

"At eight o'clock," he replied. "That is, if there is any breakfast."

"I am sure Watkins will see to that," Thelma replied lightly.

She turned towards the door.

The Earl put out his hand as if he would prevent her from going. Then he changed his mind.

As she reached the door he followed her.

The hall was in darkness except for two candles burning on a table at the foot of the stairs.

Thelma picked one of them up in her hand.

"I hope you have no ghosts in this house!"

She glanced up as she spoke at the darkness of the high ceiling.

The light thrown by the candles seemed somehow sinister.

"If you are afraid, I will come and protect you from them!" the Earl said quietly.

Thelma laughed.

"I was only teasing. I am sure there are no ghosts. In any case, even if there are, they will be your ancestors, who are longing to help you, although of course you will first have to help yourself."

She had moved up several steps of the stairs before she looked over the bannister and smiled at him.

"Perhaps to-morrow," she said, "we shall find the 'crock of gold at the end of the rainbow'. Think about that as you go to sleep!"

"I will try," the Earl answered, "but I am more likely to be thinking about you!"

Thelma laughed.

"I am quite certain, and I am prepared to take a bet on it, that you will be thinking of your animals!'

She did not wait for his answer, but ran up the last remaining steps.

Because her candle was flickering she slowed her step as she reached the landing.

As she passed into her bed-room she waved her hand to him.

He stood watching her until she was out of sight.

Then as he heard her door close firmly he went back into the Salon to extinguish the candles.

When everything was in darkness he picked up his own candle and climbed the stairs.

As he passed Thelma's door he hesitated for a moment.

Then with an effort he walked on until he reached his own room.

# Chapter Four

Thelma awoke in the morning with a feeling of expectation.

She knew that to see the menagerie of animals perform would be one of the most exciting things that had ever happened to her.

At the same time, she could not help worrying over the Earl.

How was it possible that anything so magnificent as his house and himself should be in such dire straits?

She was nervous of asking questions, but she knew that she was immensely curious.

She put on her blouse and riding-skirt and hurried down to breakfast.

Although she was early, he was already there, and he rose as she entered the Dining-Room, saying with a smile:

"I was beginning to think you really were a part of my imagination!"

"No, I am here, and actually I am very hungry!"

"You are fortunate that I have left you an egg," he said.

She thought as he handed her a plate that she had been rather tactless.

The dinner last night had certainly been very scanty.

She only hoped that Watkins would have the sense to provide something better for luncheon.

He could pay for it without the Earl being aware that he was doing so.

"As I have a great deal of work to do this morning," the

Earl said, "I suggest that, having seen the animals, you come back to the house and explore it."

"I am longing to do that," Thelma said, "but undoubtedly your menagerie comes first!"

As the Earl was casually dressed, Thelma did not collect her hat or her jacket, but rode with him to the Circus tent just as she was.

The two men she had seen before, whose names were Walter and Bill, were already busy, with Walter grooming the tigers and Bill the lions.

The animals were outside their cages, apparently content to sit while the men made a fuss of them.

As soon as the Earl appeared Sita jumped up and trotted towards him.

She put her great paws up onto his shoulders and licked his cheek.

It was a very touching sight, and Thelma wished she could make a drawing of it.

Then the Earl was giving the men instructions as to what they must do.

While he was talking, the leopard was clawing at her cage so that she could come to him.

He walked across to her and opened the door. As he stroked her she purred like a cat.

"How can he possibly destroy or even sell these beautiful creatures?" she asked herself.

Then for the first time it struck her that she could buy them.

She was rich and, whatever they might cost, it would make very little difference to her huge fortune.

Then she told herself that she had experienced an example of the Earl's pride when she had arrived.

She knew instinctively that he would resent being beholden to a woman, and especially to herself, because he thought he was protecting her.

It was a problem, but she was not prepared to worry

about it at the moment.

What was important was to get everything ready for this evening.

There were some small boys from the village who had come to look at the animals, and they were told by the Earl to clean the seats.

They were quite prepared to do anything so long as they were not sent away.

Then the Earl took Thelma to look at the monkeys who were chattering as they jumped up and down in their cage.

They were full of mischief and obviously wanted to get out.

"I have a feeling," the Earl said, "that if we once release them we should have great difficulty in getting them back in again."

"I suppose they are used to more spacious accommodation than where they are at the moment," Thelma said.

"I will show you where they are normally housed," the Earl said, "and I also want to show you my giraffe."

Having given a number of further instructions to Walter and Bill, the Earl lifted Thelma back onto *Dragonfly*.

Then he mounted his own horse and they rode away from the field where the Circus was to take place.

They went through a paddock, then into another field which lay beyond it behind a walled garden.

Here the land was divided up with partitions.

Thelma could see how carefully and cleverly the Earl had arranged his menagerie.

It was, she discovered, three years before he had gone to the Peninsula with his Regiment.

Now the long enclosures were empty.

But she could see the comfortable quarters in which the lions slept, and that they had at least half-an-acre to move about in.

The same applied to the tigers and the leopard.

There was a special enclosure for the monkeys which was

roofed over by wire netting to prevent them from jumping out.

There were trees in the centre of it which they could climb.

There were also swings to amuse them and a large, well designed hut where they could sleep.

"It looks very comfortable," Thelma said.

"I am glad that you think so," the Earl replied. "I took a lot of trouble over it, and spent a great deal of money!"

There was that sharp note in his voice which occurred whenever he mentioned money.

"Now let me see your giraffe," Thelma said quickly.

The giraffe, whose name was *Zambia*, was in an enclosure a little way from the others.

She was a very fine-looking animal, and it was fascinating for Thelma to see one for the first time.

She put out her long neck over the fence so that the Earl could feed her.

"I had planned to find a husband for *Zambia* as soon as I returned home," he said. "She was very young when I first had her. Now I suspect she will be an 'Old Maid' for the rest of her days!"

"That is another thing we have to prevent," Thelma said impulsively.

"*We*?" he asked. "Are you identifying yourself with my troubles?"

"I am not a Pharisee," Thelma explained, "and I have no intention of 'passing by on the other side'."

He smiled at her before he said:

"You cannot be real! I know I am dreaming all this!"

"Even in a dream you have to be practical," Thelma replied. "Is there anything more to see?"

He took her by the arm and drew her past the giraffe's house.

There was a pond enclosed by a railing, and she saw to her surprise that in it was a large hippopotamus.

"He will definitely not be performing to-night!" the Earl said.

"What a pity!" Thelma laughed. "I think he would be sensational!"

"Well, that is the lot!" he said in a different tone of voice. "But to amuse the guests Walter and Bill are quite good acrobats, and they have trained three of the village boys to turn somersaults. They are to be dressed up as Clowns."

"If you ask me," Thelma said, "I think the audience is getting off cheap, even at a sovereign a seat!"

"I only hope they will agree with you," the Earl replied.

She looked at him for a moment before she said:

"I think it is up to you to convince them that they are very fortunate."

She saw he did not understand, and she went on:

"I have always understood that the Master of Cere-monies is the man who makes or breaks a Circus, and no-one could look better than you in the part."

"I am not certain whether you are complimenting me, or insulting me," the Earl protested.

Thelma laughed. Then before he could assist her, she mounted *Dragonfly*.'

"I will leave you to figure it out," she said. "In the meantime, is there an Inventory of the contents of your house?"

The Earl's expression darkened.

'My cousin made sure of that!" he replied. "He had one done when I was abroad, making quite certain that every-thing was included down to the last egg-cup!"

"Where is it?" Thelma asked.

"On a table in the Library, so that I shall be constantly reminded that it exists!'

The Earl's voice was sharp and because she had no wish to upset him further, Thelma said:

"That is a challenge, and I am determined to prove your cousin wrong!"

She rode away as she spoke.

The Earl watched her go before with a sigh he mounted his own horse.

'She is very lovely!" he told himself. "For once the gods have been generous!"

Thelma found Watkins, as she expected, in the stables. As she dismounted from *Dragonfly* she said:

"I hope you have provided us with some food for luncheon."

"I've got it all fixed up, Miss Thelma!" Watkins replied.

"His Lordship must not know," she said hastily.

"Leave that t'me," Watkins answered.

As he took hold of *Dragonfly*'s bridle he said:

"If ye asks me, this place'd be all right, if it 'ad a bit o' money spent on it!"

"I agree with you," Thelma said, "but I imagine a lot of soldiers have come back from the war to find their lives in ruins."

"That's true, an' it's a cryin' shame!" Watkins replied.

He walked as he spoke into the stables. Thelma followed him.

As he put *Dragonfly* in a stall Watkins went on:

"I've bin 'earin' from the old couple in th' kitchen wot a brave man His Lordship be! Got a medal for gallantry, 'e did, 'tho that's somethin' ye can't eat!"

Thelma was silent for a moment. Then she said:

"We have to save the animals, Watkins, and I am sure you could manage to slip a number of sovereigns into the collection at the door to-night!"

"I were athinkin' th' very same thing, Miss Thelma!"

"You had better not make it too much, otherwise the Earl might become suspicious. But £10, or even £20, would not be noticeable."

Watkins nodded.

'I'll see to it, Miss, and ye'd better keep out o' sight this evenin'."

"Out of sight?" Thelma repeated in surprise.

"All them 'Nobs' from th' neighbour'ood'll be comin', from wot I hears," Watkins explained, "an' if they sees yer, Miss, they'll talk."

Thelma drew in her breath.

"Yes, of course they will! I never thought of that!"

"Ye'd better 'ide behind," Watkins went on, "'cause if anybody sees yer as knows 'er Ladyship, they might tell 'er where yer are!"

"Oh, Watkins, I am so glad you warned me!" Thelma exclaimed. "I was foolish enough to believe that we were far enough away from home for no-one to ever have heard of me."

"Ye're too pretty, Miss Thelma, an' that's th' truth!" Watkins said.

He carried *Dragonfly*'s saddle out of the stall.

Feeling there was nothing more to say, Thelma went back to the house.

She was thinking as she did so that Watkins had a great deal more sense than she had.

Of course people in the County who came to the Circus to help the Earl would be curious about her.

If they guessed he had a young woman staying with him unchaperoned, they would chatter like a lot of magpies.

'If Stepmama realises where I am, she will drag me back to marry Sir Richard!' Thelma thought in a panic.

She told herself to avoid that she would dress up as a Clown if necessary.

She went to the Library and found the Inventory.

It was where the Earl had told her it would be, on a desk just inside the door.

The Library was magnificent and there must have been at least 10,000 books in it.

There was a balcony giving access to the upper shelves, which was reached by a twisting mahogany and brass staircase.

It struck her that it might contain first editions of famous books which would be valuable.

But she knew she would not have time to search for them.

In any case, it was more than likely that the Earl's abominable cousin would have already thought of that.

She looked at the Inventory.

It was a leather-bound book with a great number of pages.

The contents of all the rooms were itemised one by one, and it was obvious that nothing had been forgotten.

She turned over the pages, trying to think where she should search first.

Then she was aware that the Inventory stopped at the Second Floor.

She supposed that the upper floors had housed the servants and there must once have been a large number of them.

Then she told herself that in a house this size there must be also attic rooms like those they had at home.

It was there that everything that was not wanted was stored.

There was just a chance that something valuable might have been put there.

Taking the Inventory with her she climbed up the main staircase.

Then there were two other staircases, which took her to the top of the house.

As she had expected, there were long rows of servants' rooms, small and furnished with iron bedsteads and deal chests-of-drawers.

In a number of the rooms the roof had been leaking and the panes of glass in the windows were so dirty that the sun could hardly percolate through them.

She went from room to room realising that her search here was hopeless.

Then when she came to the end she went down a narrow staircase which she knew would lead her to the West Wing.

This was not as high as the centre block but the rooms were all meant for guests.

They were well-furnished with exquisite French commodes, fine Chippendale furniture, or, in some cases, Elizabethan oak.

She saw at a quick glance that everything was listed on the Inventory.

She walked on feeling despairingly that she had been over-optimistic in thinking that in this way she could help the Earl.

At the far end of the West Wing was another staircase.

She went down it and found herself in what she knew must be a much older part of the house.

It had obviously been there for many generations before the renovations which had taken place at the beginning of the last century.

The walls were very thick, as thick as the Elizabethan walls at the Manor.

The rooms, which obviously had been long out of use, were small and low ceilinged.

She looked into two or three of them, then came to the Chapel.

She was not surprised, after what she had heard about the Earl's cousin, to find that it had not been used for a long time.

The dust was thick on the altar and on the carved pews.

The stained-glass window was broken in several places.

Birds had come in to make their nests on the tops of the pillars.

The cross was so tarnished that it was difficult to tell whether it was silver or gold.

Thelma stood for some minutes just looking at what had

once been a House of God.

Then she was aware that despite its appearance the atmosphere of sanctity was still there.

She moved forward to kneel in front of the altar.

Everything was very quiet and she felt as if her prayer was being heard.

"Please, God," she prayed, "let me be able to help the Earl and give him back his pride."

She remembered that when she was at School a girl who was a Catholic had told her that the Patron Saint of lost causes was St. Jude.

She had told one of the girls who wanted to pass a very difficult examination that she should pray to him.

She had done so, and passed the examination with flying colours.

Thelma thought now that the Chapel had undoubtedly been consecrated at the beginning of its long history by a Catholic Priest and later by a Protestant one.

She therefore prayed to St. Jude, hoping he would hear her.

"Please, St. Jude, let me find something . . anything that can be sold, and give the Earl the courage to go on fighting for his home and his animals."

It was a fervent prayer, for even to think of the animals being sold or destroyed made Thelma feel desperately that she must save them.

Then she suddenly heard a bird singing outside the Chapel, and she told herself it was a sign that her prayer had been heard.

She rose from her knees and saw on the right there was a curtain which she thought would lead her into the Vestry.

As she thought she might as well see everything while she was there, she pulled it aside and went into it.

There were a number of Hymn-Books and a very large Bible which should have rested on the lectern.

There was an ancient Register that had once recorded

Births, Deaths and Marriages of members of the family and the staff.

She opened it and found her hand covered with dust because it had lain untended for so long.

She left the Chapel feeling as she did so as if there was new hope in her heart.

Outside the door was a passage which she thought would run along the back of the house to join the newer building.

It was dark, but there were doors on each side of it.

She opened one and found it was a cupboard.

There were brooms and buckets ready for the house-maids to use to clean the Chapel.

She opened a door on the opposite side, then gave a little gasp.

This was what she had been seeking.

It was a long, narrow room which might once have been used as a Sitting-Room or even a School-room of some sort.

Now it was just a junk-room.

It was filled with broken pieces of furniture, packing-cases, cracked china and glass, torn cushions and faded curtains.

There was a child's rocking-horse without a tail, a dolls'-house without a roof.

There was a wicker-basket which at one time would have been strapped behind a carriage.

Thelma looked around her, feeling sure that here, although it might take time, she would find something of interest.

Then at the far end of the room she saw against the wall a whole stack of pictures.

There were big ones, small ones, some with broken frames and a great number with a cracked glass.

She had to pull them out one by one.

Some were framed maps of the estate, others were hunting-prints disfigured with damp spots, and several very ugly portraits of elderly gentlemen.

It was dispiriting, but she continued.

Then she found two pictures which seemed to her to be of interest.

They were covered with grime.

She thought they had probably been pushed in there because the strings by which they had been hung had frayed and broken.

The frames, which appeared to her to be gold and hand-carved, were now almost black.

Of one thing she was certain – they would not be on the Inventory and there was just the hope that if she cleaned them they might prove to be valuable.

She picked them up and carried them out into the passage.

In the cupboard where the housemaids' cleaning equipment was stored she found a duster. With this she cleaned away some of the dirt before she took them any further.

Then she retraced her steps to the front of the house.

It was nearly luncheontime, but there was as yet no sign of the Earl.

She put the pictures on a chair in the Library and restored the Inventory to its former place.

She decided to say nothing to the Earl about the pictures until she had had a chance to examine them more carefully.

She had no wish to raise his hopes only to have them dashed again.

She found somewhere to wash her hands, and as she returned to the Hall the Earl came hurrying up the steps.

"If I am late, you must forgive me," he said. "We had a little trouble with the horses. They like their riders sitting, not standing on their backs!"

Thelma laughed.

"Is that what Walter and Bill were trying to do?"

"They are very skilful at it," the Earl replied.

He went off to wash his hands in the cloakroom off the

Hall which Thelma had already found.

When he came back he said:

"Shall we go into the Dining-Room and look hopeful? I shall feel very embarrassed if there is nothing to eat."

"I am sure there will be something," Thelma replied confidently.

As they sat down, Watkins came hurrying in.

There was a mushroom omelette which Thelma knew he had cooked to perfection.

The Earl ate hungrily, and Thelma waited a little apprehensively to see what would come next.

She need not have worried, for there was a leg of lamb which was delicious, served with spring vegetables.

The Earl stared.

"Now where can this have come from?" he asked.

"I gets it from a farmer early this mornin', M'Lord," Watkins replied.

The Earl was about to say something when Watkins went on:

"Th' farmer asks me to say 'e 'opes M'Lord'll accept it as a present seein' as 'ow it's the first lamb to be slaughtered this year."

For a moment the Earl stiffened. Then he said:

"That is extremely kind of him, when I know they are finding things difficult, just as we all are!"

"Perhaps things will improve," Thelma remarked.

"Well, they can hardly be worse!" the Earl replied. "I find a lot of the country Banks have closed, and farmers cannot find a market for their stock."

Thelma knew that was the truth.

She thought however that it was a great mistake to talk about it.

Instead she said:

"This lamb is delicious! You must congratulate Watkins on being a very good cook!"

"I am very grateful to you," the Earl said to him. "I know

Mrs. Beale is getting too old to carry on without help, but there is nothing I can do about it."

"We're gettin' on fine, M'Lord!" Watkins replied.

When he left the room Thelma said:

"You can leave everything to Watkins – he is just like a Nanny. He takes charge of everything and it is always for one's own good!"

The Earl laughed.

"I am quite prepared to accept his help, and God knows I need it!"

"What are you doing this afternoon?' Thelma asked to change the subject.

"Getting everything ready," the Earl replied, "and that includes you! I think for you just to be seen on *Dragonfly* will give the Circus the *finesse* it lacks at the moment!"

There was silence. Then Thelma said:

'I . . I am sorry . . but I cannot appear."

"Why not?"

"You guessed . . the reason last . . night."

"That you are in hiding?"

He looked down at her in a puzzled fashion before he said:

"Surely you do not think anybody who may come here to-night will recognise you?"

From the way he spoke it flashed through Thelma's mind that he did not think that she had any social standing.

It was something that had never crossed her mind.

Then she realised that if she was a Lady in the full meaning of the word, she would not be riding about the countryside accompanied only by a groom.

She had tried to pretend that she was a married woman.

The Earl however had quickly exploded that idea, because she was not wearing a wedding-ring.

"Then what did he think?" she asked herself.

She was too innocent to guess the truth.

She only supposed that he thought her to be someone

from London, which would account for her smart riding-habit, or perhaps he thought her to be an actress.

Whatever it was, she would obviously not be known to the County families who would support him this evening.

Because he was waiting for an explanation she said:

"I have admitted that I am in hiding, but even if your friends do not recognise me, suppose they talk? They would certainly think it strange that I was staying with you."

"Yes, of course, I had not thought of that," the Earl said. "I suppose *Dragonfly* would not qualify as a Chaperon?"

He laughed at his own joke, and Thelma said:

'I am sure he would be a very strict one. So if you want *Dragonfly* to perform, which he is longing to do, you must ride him!"

There was no mistaking the light in the Earl's eyes as he asked:

"Do you really mean that?"

"I could not deny *Dragonfly* the applause he would so much enjoy, and I am sure you will look like Apollo on him!"

"Now I shall definitely accept your offer," the Earl said, "but I could not bear you to miss the performance."

"I will watch from the back,' Thelma said. "What time is your audience invited?"

"At five o'clock, which means the performance will take place in daylight, and they will be home in time for dinner."

Thelma laughed.

"I see you have thought it out carefully."

"I want the money," the Earl said, "and that is the best time of day, when they will have no other engagements."

There was some excellent cheese to eat after the lamb.

Lastly a pot of hot coffee which compensated the Earl for having nothing else to drink but water.

"An excellent meal!" he said as he finished. "I feel ready for anything!"

"The 'orses be waitin' outside, M'Lord," Watkins said coming into the room, "an' I've brought round both *Dragonfly* and *Juno*."

He looked at Thelma as he spoke and she said to the Earl:

"What Watkins is saying is that you must ride *Dragonfly* and get to know him."

"That is something I am only too willing to do!" the Earl answered.

The Earl mounted *Dragonfly* having assisted Thelma onto *Juno's* saddle.

They rode quickly down to the tent while Watkins followed on an inferior horse.

Walter and Bill were leading the cheetahs round the ring.

The beautiful animals soon found it boring and tried to escape.

When they were unable to do so, they protested angrily until they were put back into their cage.

It was amusing to watch them struggling with their keepers and Thelma said:

"If they do that to-night, it will be a very popular turn!"

The Earl smiled.

"That is what I was thinking. They are not professionals and never will be, but the unexpected is invariably entertaining."

"You are so clever that you ought to take this up as a living!" Thelma teased.

"I am quite ready to do that, if you will come into partnership with me," the Earl replied.

It struck Thelma that it would be a very amusing thing to do.

But she knew that what he really wanted was to live as his father and grandfather had lived in the big house with servants to wait on him.

And of course with his stables filled with superlative horses.

Once again she was praying that she could help him, but knew at the same time that it was not going to be easy.

Walter and Bill together with the Earl then took the other animals round the ring to get them used to it.

After that the men were sent to fetch the giraffe and the Earl looked at his watch.

"I think I should go and get ready," he said to Thelma.

"Yes, of course," she agreed, "and as I am not going to perform I will stay here in the tent."

He smiled his agreement, and mounted *Dragonfly* to ride back to the house.

Watkins went with him to fetch some of the clothes that were required.

"The boys should be along shortly," the Earl said to Thelma as he rode off.

She watched him go and thought how magnificently he rode. He should never have to ride a horse that was not as fine as *Dragonfly*.

She went behind the tent and started to sort out the Clowns' costumes which were in a crate, together with various other clothing.

All of them had been left behind with the rest of the Circus equipment.

She thought some of the clothes should have been washed and pressed, but it was too late to do anything about that now.

She arranged them in neat piles so that those who had to wear them could put them on as quickly as possible.

There was only about half-an-hour before the boys from the village were expected, and Walter and Bill had not yet come back with the giraffe.

Suddenly a strange voice beside her asked:

"Who are you?"

She looked up and saw a man very elegantly dressed. In fact he was almost a 'Dandy'.

His tight champagne-coloured breeches fitted closely

and without a wrinkle.

His Hessian boots shone as if they had been polished with champagne.

The points of his collar over his intricately-tied cravat were high above his chin.

He was however not a handsome man, and he looked to Thelma to be about forty years old.

There was a touch of grey at his temples and she thought he had a debauched look.

His eyes seemed to rove over her in an impertinent manner.

In answer to his question she said:

"I might ask, Sir, who you are!"

"I am, if you are interested," he replied, "Cyril Mere, and as a member of the family, I wish to know what is going on here!"

Thelma gave an audible gasp.

This morning when she had been looking at the Inventory she had read what was on the front cover. It read:

> *"AN INVENTORY OF MERSTONE HOUSE COMPILED IN JULY, 1814 ON THE INSTRUCTIONS OF CYRIL MERE ESQUIRE."*

Now she knew that the man standing beside her was the cousin and Heir Presumptive to the Earl, who had allowed the house to deteriorate into such an appalling state.

She drew herself up to face him before she said slowly and distinctly:

"I think, Mr. Mere, your information should come from the Earl of Merstone, who will be returning here in a few minutes."

"Are you telling me that this vulgar Circus is his doing?" Cyril Mere enquired.

He looked around him disdainfully. Then his eyes came back to her.

"And of course," he said, "there is no need to ask what part you play!"

He paused for a moment as if he expected her to answer.

As she only faced him defiantly he went on:

"You are far too pretty to be wasting yourself and your charms here. I can assure you you will receive no payment for them!"

Cyril Mere eyed her in a manner she thought definitely insulting.

"I suggest, Mr. Mere," she said in a voice that she hoped was as scathing as her feelings, "that you mind your own business and let me get on with mine. If you wish to see the Circus, you will have to pay for your seat!"

She turned away from him with a little flounce as she spoke.

She walked quickly out of the tent to stand beside the lions' cage as if she thought they afforded her some protection.

Slowly, as if he was asserting his authority, Cyril Mere walked after her.

When he saw where she was standing, he hesitated as if he was debating with himself whether he should continue to speak to her or ignore her for her rudeness.

He decided on the latter.

Without raising his hat he walked away to where just beyond some trees Thelma could see a closed carriage was waiting.

It was a very smart vehicle drawn by two well-bred horses with a coachman on the box and a footman standing at the door.

Cyril Mere stepped into it without looking back.

As he got into it she saw that the Merstone coat-of-arms was emblazoned on the door.

She knew how that would infuriate the Earl because it was something to which his cousin was not entitled.

Then as Cyril Mere drove away she decided she would

there was one wrapped in a towel at the bottom of the basket.

She propped it up on a packing-case and pulled on the wig which had elastic to keep it in place.

It was really rather becoming in a vulgar sort of way.

Because she thought it would make the Earl laugh, she made up her face with the grease-paint and powder that she had put ready for the Clowns.

There was also a blackpencil with which she outlined her eyes and eye-brows.

"No-one would recognise me now," she told her reflection in the mirror.

She was staring at herself when Watkins came to join her.

"I've bin thinkin', Miss Thelm . . ." he began.

Then as she turned round he exclaimed.

"Th' Lord love us! Wot 'ave yer done to yerself?"

"I have found a way of taking part in the Circus!" Thelma replied. "I do not see why everybody else should have all the fun!"

Watkins laughed.

"Well, yer certainly looks th' part, Miss!"

"Are you quite sure no-one would recognise me?" Thelma asked a little anxiously.

"I've got th' answer to that," Watkins said. "I finds it when I were alookin' for a hat for Walter."

He searched among the crates and came back with a small mask for her eyes.

It was obviously meant for a woman or perhaps a young boy.

He handed it to Thelma who put it on, and when she looked in the mirror she said:

"An excellent disguise! Now all I have to do is persuade His Lordship to let me take part."

"I've got a good idea, Miss," Watkins said.

After Thelma had listened to it she clapped her hands.

"Watkins, you are a genius! Of course that is exactly what we should do to start the performance."

"Wot I really comes to say was," Watkins said, "it'd be wise if I took th' money at th' door. There be no-one else, an' it'd be a mistake to trust 'em villagers."

"Of course, you are right."

Lowering her voice she added:

"Do not forget what I suggested."

"I 'as it in me pocket," Watkins answered.

At that moment the boys who would be playing the part of the Clowns came running in.

Watkins helped them dress while Thelma tactfully went into the Ring.

She was counting how many seats there were when she saw the Earl dismounting from *Dragonfly*.

As he came towards her she thought that no one could look better for the part he was playing.

He was wearing black knee-breeches and silk stockings.

Instead of his cut-away evening coat, he wore one of 'hunting pink', which had a velvet collar.

His cravat was as smart as if he was going to Carlton House to see the Prince Regent.

On the side of his head he had, as was traditional, a high-crowned hat.

"You look wonderful!" Thelma exclaimed as he entered the tent.

Then she realised he was staring at her in sheer astonishment.

The expression on his face was ludicrous as she bent her knees in the correct manner of a Ballerina.

"May I introduce myself? I am the Spirit of the Circus, come to bring you luck!"

"You mean you are going to appear?" the Earl asked in an incredulous voice.

'I am going to ride *Juno*,' Thelma replied.

"You will certainly improve my programme," the Earl said. "At the same time, do you think it is wise? It may cause a lot of gossip."

"I have thought of that," Thelma answered in a serious tone. "Should your friends ask any questions, as they undoubtedly will, you can say that I am a local girl who offered to help and you know little about me."

The Earl smiled.

"I hope they will believe me!"

"Be convincing!" Thelma admonished him.

There was very little time left before Walter and Bill were dressed in their costumes.

The clowns were rushing about the ring with excitement and Watkins took up his place at the entrance.

He had, Thelma noticed with amusement, a saddle-bag in which to put the money.

She only hoped there would be a lot to fill it.

Because she thought it was important that she should not be seen until the performance started, she went behind to peep through the red curtain that led into the ring.

The first arrival was a nice-looking couple whom the Earl was obviously pleased to see.

"It is delightful to have you back amongst us, Merstone," the Gentleman said, "and as you are doing this for your animals, I told my man to put the carcass of an ox we have just killed in the larder at the house."

"That is extremely kind of you," the Earl said.

As other people kept arriving, Thelma knew that they were all aware of the conditions the Earl had found on his return from the war.

One man had brought him a case of wine, another lady told him she had two chickens for him in her carriage.

Another arrival, who was a Countess, told him he would find two of her guinea-fowls loose in front of the house.

"They are better than any guard-dog, my dear boy!" she said. "As you are alone, I feel you need protection!"

"That is really very kind of you," the Earl said, "and I am very grateful!"

More and more people arrived.

A great number had felt that they must bring something to show the Earl they appreciated him.

Thelma thought it was because of his record of gallantry as a soldier.

She was also quite certain they disliked his cousin.

It would have been impossible for the people in the County not to be aware that Cyril Mere had, while the Earl was away, allowed the house and the estate to go to rack and ruin.

It would have been surprising if they had not been suspicious that he was spending money to which he was not entitled.

"In the country, everything becomes known," Thelma told herself, "and gossip is carried by the birds and the bees."

She could see while she was watching that the Earl was looking really happy. He had not expected his friends and neighbours to remember him so generously.

'This is just what he needs,' Thelma thought.

She calculated that, as the Earl came back to start the performance, there were sixty people in the tent.

Walter was holding *Dragonfly* and *Juno* for them, while Bill had decorated their bridles with flowers.

The Earl helped Thelma into the saddle and she sat elegantly, her leg over the pommel, her ballet skirt spread out.

Then he mounted *Dragonfly*.

As he did so one of the boys from the village beat a drum.

"Here we go!" the Earl said to Thelma, and he was laughing.

They entered the ring and there was a round of applause.

They circled it three times until they stopped in the middle.

"Ladies and Gentlemen," the Earl began, "we intend to show you this evening a number of the magnificent animals which form the Merstone Menagerie. We hope you will appreciate their performance, just as they appreciate your being here this evening."

He swept off his hat as he finished speaking and Thelma made *Juno* bow in the way that Watkins had taught her to do.

To loud applause they trotted round the ring again then out through the exit.

Now it was time for the Clowns to show their paces and the boys from the village turned somersaults one after another.

The Earl went into the ring to make jokes about them while Walter and Bill tied up the horses and got ready to introduce the lions.

From the very beginning Thelma thought that everything went smoothly.

The lions and the tigers behaved with dignity and looked so magnificent doing so that they received huge rounds of applause.

The cheetahs staged a protest which was amusing because it was entirely natural.

The monkeys were a nuisance which made everybody laugh.

They climbed up the poles of the tent, they jumped onto the empty seats.

Then into the laps of the spectators, some of whom were nervous of them.

They tumbled about on the ground and made it very difficult for Walter and Bill to catch them.

Finally they were back in their cage when the Earl and the Clowns had kept everybody amused and laughing for quite a long time.

Then the last two stars of the show were to appear.

It was the Earl who had thought that nothing would be

more dramatic than that the audience should see together the dark sensuous beauty of the leopard, and the high-necked elegance of the giraffe.

As they were led round the ring Thelma was certain that a great number of the people, like herself, had never seen a giraffe before.

The leopard was so beautiful that she was sure no Lady could rival her.

Only when they had left the ring did the Earl and Thelma go back again.

They rode their horses round and round as fast as they dared.

Then the Earl made a final speech.

He thanked everybody for coming and said that in doing so they had prolonged the lives of the animals.

He could now keep them alive for much longer than he had dared to hope.

There was a little gasp among the audience as they realised what he had said.

Many of them had been aware that he could not afford to keep his menagerie.

But to hear him say bluntly that they would have had to be destroyed was a shock.

As soon as they realised the performance was over the audience left their seats and stepped into the Ring to speak to the Earl.

Tactfully Thelma disappeared.

Watkins, leaving the entrance, took hold of *Dragonfly*'s bridle as the Earl dismounted, and led him round behind.

"Will ye take *Dragonfly* back, Miss Thelma?" he asked. "I've got a feeling, after wot 'Is Lordship said, as there'll be a few more sovereigns being 'anded out as 'is friends leave."

Thelma realised this was a sensible idea.

She bent to pick up her riding-skirt and blouse which she had left on a packing-case.

She went out by the back way and started riding towards the house.

It would be easier for the Earl, if he was asked, to explain away her presence if she was not there.

Apart from the fact that this was his glorious hour, and she did not want to spoil it.

'Now that he realises that people will co-operate with him,' she thought, 'he will not be so much on edge.'

She put *Dragonfly* in his stall, taking off his bridle and saddle.

Then she went into the house.

She went upstairs to her room and looked at her reflection in the mirror.

It was easier to see herself here than in the tent.

She thought with amusement that no-one who had seen her would have the least idea that she was a Lady and a débutante.

She pulled off her wig, then realised that it must be nearly seven o'clock.

She must eventually put on one of her muslin gowns in which to dine with the Earl.

She expected however that dinner would be late, for Watkins would not leave if there was a chance of getting any more money from the Earl's more generous friends.

There was therefore no hurry.

She put on a light muslin wrap that she had brought with her, and went into the Boudoir next to her bed-room and sat down to look at the pictures she had found in the Lumber-room.

She was almost certain as she had been at first that they were by a Master artist.

If so they would be valuable.

Because she was excited by the idea, she began very

carefully to clean one of them and take off a great deal of the dirt.

There was a knock on the door.

"Come in!" she called.

As she expected, it was Watkins.

He entered the room and put the saddle-bag down on a chair.

"There's over a 'undred in that," he said proudly, "a 'undred yeller ones!"

Thelma gave a little cry of excitement.

"I do not believe it! Oh, Watkins, how wonderful!"

"They nearly all gives a bit more before they goes," Watkins grinned. "Do yer still want me to do wot yer suggested, Miss Thelma?"

"Yes, of course," Thelma said.

"Then that be £122!"

Thelma looked at the saddle-bag then at his face, and he asked:

"Shall I tell His Lordship, or will ye?"

'Let me tell him," Thelma said, her eyes shining.

"I think 'e'll be a bit longer," Watkins said, "but we'll 'ave somewat t' eat, including an ox, if us needs it!"

Thelma laughed.

"I am sure that would be very tough."

"There's plenty without that," Watkins answered, then he was gone.

Thelma walked across the room to look into the saddle-bag.

She could hardly believe they had been so successful and she said a little prayer of thankfulness.

There was a knock on the door and the Earl came in.

She turned towards him eagerly. To her surprise he put his finger to his lips.

"What is it?" she asked in a whisper.

"I could not do anything about it," he answered, "but two of my friends insisted on coming back with me for dinner, thinking I was alone."

Thelma made a little murmur, and he went on:

"They have actually brought the food with them because they were aware of the conditions here."

"I understand," Thelma said, "and I will keep out of sight."

"I am very sorry," the Earl said. "I was looking forward to our dining together."

"So was I," Thelma admitted, "but I have something exciting to tell you."

He did not speak as Thelma indicated with her hand the saddle-bag lying on the chair.

"One hundred and twenty two pounds!" she said slowly.

"I do not believe it!"

"It is true!"

The Earl drew in his breath. Then he said:

"You have certainly brought me luck – a luck I never expected would be mine."

She looked at him as he spoke, and as she met his eyes she had the strange feeling that it was impossible to move.

At the same time she felt as if the Earl was pulling her towards him.

Then there was the sound of men's voices in the distance.

It seemed to break the spell that she had felt between them, although what it was Thelma was not quite sure.

"I must go," the Earl said, "and we will talk about it when they have gone."

He smiled at her.

Opening the door he went out into the corridor and shut it quietly behind him.

A moment later she heard him say:

"I am just going to change my coat. Go into the Salon."

"We want some glasses," a man's voice answered.

"You will have to look for them in the Pantry," the Earl replied.

Then Thelma heard him moving towards the Master

Bed-room at the end of the corridor, and because she thought it sensible, she locked her door.

She was disappointed, very disappointed that she could not dine with the Earl.

They had so much to talk about, so much to say to each other. She could only hope that his guests would not stay long.

Very much later, Watkins brought her dinner on a tray.

She knew he would have served the Earl and his guests in the Dining-Room, and he was only able to come to her when he had finished.

By this time she was too tired to go on working on the picture.

She just sat at the window watching the stars coming out, and a half-moon moving up the sky.

"I couldn't get 'ere any earlier, Miss Thelma," Watkins apologised as she unlocked the door to let him in. 'Them gent'men 'ad brought enough with 'em to feed a Regiment! We won't be goin' 'ungry for another week!"

"That is good news!" Thelma replied.

"I've brought yer a little bit of most things," Watkins explained, "and a glass o' champagne."

"Which I shall enjoy," Thelma smiled.

"If yer takes my advice, Miss Thelma," Watkins went on, "you'll nip into bed an' get some sleep. Them downstairs 'll be laughing and drinkin' 'til th' early hours, I shouldn't wonder!"

Thelma felt her heart sink.

She had so longed to be with the Earl.

She told herself it was just because they had the success of the Circus to talk and laugh about, but she knew too that she felt lonely and neglected.

"I am being ridiculous!" she told herself.

She tried to enjoy the pâté, the freshly cooked tongue, and a number of other delicacies which Watkins had brought up to her.

There was a trifle, heavily laced with sherry, with which she drank the champagne.

When she had finished, it made her more sleepy than she was already.

It had been a long day, one way and another, and she had worked very hard getting the costumes ready.

Because she was so anxious that it should be a success, that had been tiring too.

Finally, when it was long after midnight, she took Watkins' advice and leaving the Gentlemen went to bed.

She left the curtains open so that she could see the stars.

Not very long after she was in bed her eyes closed, and she was asleep.

She did not wake when an hour later the Earl came in very quietly.

He had undressed and was wearing a long robe which reached the ground, and he was carrying a candle in his hand.

In the light of it he could see Thelma quite clearly.

She looked young and very lovely with her fair hair falling over her shoulders and her hands resting outside the sheets.

He shut the door and put down the candle, and stood looking at her.

There was so much he wanted to say to her; so much he had not said last night because she had been tired.

Now she looked so beautiful that he longed to get into bed beside her and take her in his arms.

Then he thought she might be frightened.

He was quite certain she must be far more sophisticated than she appeared to be.

No-one who was really young and innocent would be riding about the countryside alone.

At the same time, he remembered how frightened she

had looked when he had raged at her when she first arrived.

He did not wish her to be frightened now and he hesitated.

In the moonlight she looked almost like a young angel who had fallen out of Heaven by mistake.

It was late and it had been a long day. There was tomorrow and a great number of days after that.

The Earl bent forward.

Very gently his lips touched Thelma's.

Then as she did not stir he picked up his candle and went from the room.


Thelma was dreaming that *Juno* was dancing round the ring, but instead of applauding the audience was chattering.

They were talking about her and pointing to her, asking who she was.

She awoke with a start and realised she was in bed and the moonlight was shining through the window.

It was then she was aware of a noise she thought had only been in her dreams but which she now realised came from the guinea-fowl which the Earl had been given as a present.

She could hear them clucking noisily outside and wondered what could have disturbed them.

She got out of bed.

The guinea-fowl were still annoyed at something and as she looked out of the window it was at first difficult to focus her eyes because she was still half-asleep.

Then she saw that behind some shrubs, which untended had grown tall and untidy, something was moving.

She thought at first it was an animal, or rather three of them.

Then she saw there were two men, and they were dragging something between them which looked like a large box.

She could not imagine what they could be doing.

As they moved a little further to the side she watched them breathlessly.

Then coming up the incline towards the house was another man.

For a moment she just glanced at him. Then she stiffened and looked again.

She was almost certain it was Cyril Mere.

There was something in the way he moved elegantly and disdainfully, the way in which he spread his feet which made her sure it was him.

She had seen him only briefly that morning, but because she had disliked him so violently she knew now she could identify him.

He seemed to be keeping in the shadows. Now the two men had set down the box on the ground.

"What can they be doing?" Thelma asked herself.

She found it very puzzling.

She wondered if the Earl was aware that his cousin was snooping round the house, and was sure that if he knew it would infuriate him.

One of the men who had been dragging the box now held something in his hand.

He looked as if he was holding a football, although she could not believe it was one.

He had moved from where he was standing and now began to walk towards the front-door.

As he did so he squeezed what he held in his hand, and something dripped from it down onto the ground.

Thelma told herself it was so incomprehensible that she must be dreaming.

Inclining her head, she could see the man going up the steps to the front-door, squeezing all the time what he held.

A second later she could not see what he was doing for he had disappeared from her view.

Then as he reappeared, walking back towards the other man by the box, she saw that he no longer held the 'football' in his hand.

It was then, mingled with the sounds of the guinea-fowl, which were still clucking some distance away, that she heard a different sound.

It came from the box.

Incredibly she realised it was the snarl of an animal.

It did not sound very ferocious until she saw that the men were bending down behind the box, deliberately inciting the animal to anger.

The sounds the animal was making then became more aggressive, and it was snarling.

The snarling then turned to yelps, as if the animal was in pain.

It was so loud that she was sure that the Earl must hear it.

She tried to look along the side of the house towards his window to see if he was looking out.

As she did so she realised that while she could see the men and the box, the bushes would have obscured the Earl's view.

Suddenly with a perception that flashed like a shaft of lightning Thelma knew what Cyril Mere was planning.

She turned from the window, and running across her room she pulled open the door.

She was only just in time, for hurrying down the corridor was the Earl.

He had obviously got out of bed and dressed hurriedly.

He was wearing only a shirt and a long black trousers. His feet were in bed-room slippers.

She moved towards him and he said hastily:

"It is all right! One of my animals must have escaped and is in pain."

Thelma put out her hand and was holding him by the shirt.

"It is . . not one of . . your animals," she said breath-

98

lessly. "It is a . . trap set for . . you by your . . cousin Cyril!"

The Earl who had been moving despite the fact that she was holding onto him, stopped still.

"What are you saying?" he asked.

"Two men have brought an . . animal in a . . cage and have . . hidden it in the bushes!"

She gave a little gasp as she said:

"I know now that they have put a . . piece of meat on the . . front-door. When you open it they will . . release the tiger . . or whatever animal it is . . and it . . will attack . . you!"

"I think you must be dreaming!" the Earl said.

"Come and look for yourself!" Thelma said. "But for God's sake, do not go out through the front-door!"

In answer, the Earl ran down the stairs and Thelma followed him.

It was easy to see their way because high windows in the hall admitted the moonlight.

He went to a window and looked out.

He could see from there behind the bushes and he saw that Thelma had told him the truth.

He could recognise an animal's cage, and crouching behind it were two men.

Thelma was at his side.

"Now you can see the trail of blood from the meat," she said in a whisper.

It was there, extending from the bushes across the gravel in front of the steps.

The Earl's lips tightened.

Then before he could speak, he saw the men almost doubled up in their anxiety not to be seen moving away down the grass incline.

They had opened the cage and a tiger was coming out!

Thelma made a little murmur of horror.

It was a large and very ferocious-looking tiger, unlike the

Earl's, and she could see it was thin, the bones of its body standing out.

With its nose to the ground it quickly picked up the scent of the blood.

Then with great bounds it was up the steps and jumping up violently at the front-door.

The man must have put the meat up very high for it sprang and went on springing, its claws scratching the wood.

It was making as it did so terrifying noises.

"Stay there!" the Earl said sharply.

He moved to one side and Thelma thought in horror that he intended to open the front-door.

Instead he ran down the hall and she knew he was going down the passage which led to the kitchen.

For a moment she could not imagine what he could be doing.

She could only wait, feeling paralysed with fear by the sounds the tiger was making.

Although she knew it was impossible, she was afraid that he might somehow break down the door.

Then the Earl was back and she saw he carried something large in his hands.

She could not see what it was in the darkness of the hall.

When he reached her side the moonlight revealed that it was a leg of a large animal.

She knew then it came from the ox that he had been given by one of his friends.

The Earl opened the window opposite her and moving very quietly he flung the ox's leg out onto the gravel.

The tiger was making so much noise that Thelma thought if there had been anybody else on that side of the house besides themselves, he would undoubtedly have woken them up.

The Earl had thrown the ox's leg so that it landed at the bottom of the steps.

They could not see the tiger, but Thelma thought it must have been drawn to the sound of it falling, and instinct told it what it was.

In one great bound the tiger jumped from the top of the steps onto the leg.

He started tearing at it frantically, as if he had not eaten for a long time.

Thelma gave a deep sigh.

She had saved the Earl.

If he had gone, as he had intended, to open the door and find out what was happening outside, the tiger would have killed him.

For a moment she felt a pain that was sheer relief.

She put her hand out to the Earl, but instead of taking it, he put his arm round her.

"Wait!" he said, and it was an order.

He was looking out of the window.

As if he could see what he expected, he pulled the curtains on either side of them so that they were in shadow.

Then his arm tightened and Thelma was aware that he was watching the three men who were approaching the house.

Ahead walked Cyril Mere, the other two were some paces behind him.

There was an air of jauntiness about Cyril Mere's approach.

It told Thelma without words what he was expecting to find, and what he had planned with a diabolical cleverness.

The tiger was still gnawing at the ox's leg.

Then just as Cyril Mere reached the top of the incline the moon was temporarily obscured by a cloud.

It made it hard to see anything low on the ground.

Cyril Mere stood at the edge of the grass and Thelma watching was aware that he was peering at the tiger.

She could not see, but she felt sure there was a smile of satisfaction on his lips.

He moved further forward. He was ready, she thought, to identify the Earl whose death he had planned so cleverly.

It flashed through her mind that if the Earl had been killed by a tiger, no-one would think for a moment it was not one from his own menagerie.

Cyril Mere still advanced.

Now there was no mistaking the manner in which he walked, and the angle of his hat with its curled brim.

He stopped several yards from the tiger, and for the first time the animal became aware of him.

He let out a low, ferocious growl and moved protectively in front of the leg, as if to be sure it could not be taken from him.

Cyril Mere moved only his head trying to see what was on the ground behind the tiger.

It was then that the animal sprang.

It was so quick, so unexpected, that it was impossible for Cyril Mere to defend himself.

The tiger knocked him over backwards.

He fell with a horrifying scream to the ground, and as he did so his hat fell off.

Then the animal's teeth were in his neck.

The other two men who were still a few paces behind, were only aware of what was happening when it was far too late to do anything about it.

One of them fumbled in his pocket, but it was several seconds later before he could fire a pistol.

The explosion seemed to echo round the house and away into the Park.

It made Thelma start convulsively.

Because she had been mesmerised by what was happening, she turned her head to hide her face against the Earl.

His arm tightened round her.

Then the two men outside, realising the danger they were in, started to run.

They tore down the grass and through the trees to the

carriage belonging to the man who had paid them.

It was impossible to see them.

But as the Earl rushed to open the front-door he could hear the sound of wheels and horses' hoofs as they drove away.

He had left Thelma sitting in the window.

As he took his arm from her she had covered her face with her hands.

The Earl went out through the front-door and looked up at the meat which had attracted the tiger and which had been thrown up onto a ledge over the door where the animal could not reach it.

He walked down the steps.

One look at what lay on the gravel revealed the dying tiger, its muscles still twitching as life ebbed slowly from him.

Beneath the animal was his cousin with his neck and face half torn away.

The Earl turned back and went through the front-door, pushing it to behind him.

He saw that Thelma was still crouching where he had left her.

He bent down and picked her up in his arms.

As he did so, she made a frightened little murmur and hid her face against his shoulder.

"It is all over," he said quietly, "and you have been very brave!"

He carried her up into her bed-room and put her down on the bed.

"You heard nothing, you have seen nothing, and you know nothing!" he said gently.

As he took his arms away from her, Thelma spoke for the first time.

"You . . are safe . . they have not . . hurt you!"

There was something desperate in the way she spoke.

The Earl bent over her.

"I am alive," he said, "and thank you, my darling, for saving me!"

For a moment his lips rested against hers.

Then before she could realise what was happening, he was gone and the door had shut behind him.

# Chapter Six

When the Earl had gone, Thelma realised that he had kissed her.

She lay looking at the stars outside in the sky, thinking it was the most wonderful thing that had ever happened.

She had known before that her whole body vibrated towards him.

When she had prayed for him in the Chapel, it had been a prayer that came from the very depths of her heart.

But somehow until this moment she had not thought of him as a man who would be attracted to her and who would love her.

Now she knew she wanted more than anything in the whole world to have the Earl's love.

Of course she loved him!

How could she not do so when he was different from any other man she had ever met, and so attractive that he was like a Greek god?

Apart from that, there was something within herself that responded to everything the Earl said, to every movement he made and now to his lips.

"I love . . him!" she told the stars and thought despairingly that he would never love her.

He had kissed her, but it had been the gentle kiss that a man might give a child.

"I am too young, too inexperienced for him," she told herself. "Besides which, he would never contemplate

105

loving anybody, considering the position he is in at the moment."

Somehow, she thought, she must persuade him to let her stay, and she could manage, with Watkins' help, to see they did not cost him anything.

At least the animals in the menagerie would be saved, but she knew the Earl wanted far more than that.

He wanted his house to be as magnificent again as it had been in his father's and grandfather's time.

She had money, but how could she tell the Earl how rich she was?

She knew if she did so she would strike at his pride and make him more aggressive about his poverty than he was already.

She turned the problem over and over in her mind until without meaning to she fell asleep.

Thelma awoke with a start to realise the Earl was standing beside her bed.

As she looked up at him he sat down on the mattress facing her.

He had not brought a candle with him but now the dawn was breaking.

He was silhouetted against the translucent gold of the rising sun.

Its light was moving slowly into the room and, while it was still hard for her to see his face, he could see hers.

"You look very lovely in the morning," he said gently.

Everything that had occurred came back to Thelma's mind and she gave a little gasp.

"W . what has . . happened?" she asked. "What . . have you . . done?"

The Earl reached out and took her hand in his.

"Watkins helped me to move my cousin's body into the house," he said, "and now he has gone to the village to collect the Doctor and find out if there is a coffin into which

Cyril's body can be put as quickly as possible."

His voice deepened as he added:

"He is not a pretty sight, and the fewer people who see him the better!"

Thelma's fingers tightened on the Earl's.

"Now . . you are . . safe!" she whispered.

"I am safe, and it is entirely thanks to you," he replied. "If you had not stopped me from opening the front-door, I would have gone out thinking that one of my tigers was in pain."

"It was the guinea-fowl which woke me," Thelma murmured.

"I think it was also your prayers," the Earl said unexpectedly.

He could see her eyes were shining in the first rays of the morning sun.

"What I am going to do now,' he said, "is to ride *Dragonfly*, if you will let me, to the house of the Chief Constable. It is only a few miles from here, if I go across the fields."

"Of course you must ride *Dragonfly*,' Thelma agreed, "but will you be . . long?"

There was a wistfulness about the question which told the Earl she wanted to be with him.

"I am afraid," he said quietly, "that once I have informed the Chief Constable, the Doctor, and a number of other people who must also be contacted, what has happened, you will have to stay out of sight."

He knew she was disappointed, and added:

"What I want more than anything else is to stay here and tell you how lovely you are, but there is a great deal to do before I am free to do that."

She looked at him in surprise and as she did so, he bent forward. He put his arms around her and held her closely against him.

His lips were on hers, and now he was kissing her very differently from how he had last night.

His kiss was fierce, demanding and possessive, and it took Thelma by surprise.

At the same time she thought something wonderful awoke within her.

It was as if the spirit of Life moved through her body and vibrated from her lips to his.

The Earl's lips became even more demanding.

As she surrendered herself completely to the wonder of them he moved one arm from around her shoulders.

She felt his hand on her breast.

Because it was so unexpected and because she could feel the strength of his fingers through the thin material of her nightgown, she instinctively put up her hands to press him away from her.

"No! Please . . no!"

She was not quite certain what she was asking.

She only knew in some way she did not understand that she was frightened of his feelings and of her own.

As she spoke, the Earl stiffened.

Then slowly he took his lips from hers and raised his head to look down at her.

He did not speak and after a moment Thelma said in a very small voice:

"P . please . . you must not . . touch me . . like that!"

The Earl was very still.

He took his other arm from around her and straightened himself.

Because she thought she was losing him Thelma put out her hands to hold onto him.

"I . . love you," she said, "but we must not . . do anything . . that is . . wrong."

The Earl was still silent, and she looked at him a little piteously.

He could see her eyes very clearly in the pale light which now seemed to fill the room.

"We will talk about it later in the day," he said, and his voice was very deep. "Now I must go to the Chief Constable, and meantime you must not let anybody see you."

He rose as he spoke and although her hands went out to him he did not seem to see them.

"Take care of yourself," he said as he reached the door.

He went from the room without looking back.

Thelma gave a little cry to stop him, but it was too late.

She could hear his footsteps going along the passage to the top of the stairs.

Then the feeling of ecstasy he had given her swept over her again.

He had kissed her and until this moment she had never known how wonderful a kiss could be.

"I love him . . I love . . him!" she said aloud, and felt as if the sunshine blinded her eyes.


A little later Thelma got up and dressed.

She was just arranging her hair in the mirror when there was a knock on the door and Watkins came in with her breakfast on a tray.

'Oi thought yer'd be awake, Miss Thelma.'

He held the tray on one hand, and shut the door with the other.

"'Ere's yer breakfast," he said as he put the tray down on a table. "His Lordship's orders is that yer're to lock yer door an' keep out o' sight."

"Is His Lordship back?" Thelma asked eagerly.

"Not yet," Watkins replied, "but there's plenty of people messin' about in th' house already, an' there'll be a lot more afore we're finished!"

"What sort of people?" Thelma enquired.

"There's the Doctor and th' village carpenter who's gone to get a coffin 'e's half finished for somebody else, an' a number of 'Nosey Parkers' from th' village as knows that somethin's up an' wants to find out what it is!"

Watkins spoke in a way which made Thelma want to laugh.

At the same time, she felt what had happened was too serious to be treated lightly.

"They tells me," Watkins went on as if he could not keep the information to himself, "that this 'ere tiger as was killed were so dangerous that no-one in th' Circus he came from would go near 'im."

Thelma could understand that was exactly why Cyril Mere had bought him.

She was however not certain how much the Earl would have told Watkins of what had occurred, and thought it best to say nothing.

"Now, yer eat yer breakfast while it's 'ot," Watkins said, "an' I'll come back an' tell ye what's 'appening, so yer won't feel left out o' things."

He grinned as he spoke.

When he had left the room Thelma sat down to a breakfast of eggs and bacon, and coffee that was hot and excellent.

She felt sure that Watkins had bought it in the village with her money.

It was unlikely that the Earl would have purchased anything so expensive.

While she ate she was worrying as to how she could help him without striking at his pride or even making him suspicious.

As she felt constrained and imprisoned in her rooms, beautiful though they were, she thought the best thing she could do was to go on cleaning the pictures.

Perhaps by a miracle her prayers would be answered, and they would prove to be as valuable as she hoped.

She had half-cleaned one yesterday.

Now when she went into the Boudoir she could see what

looked like the head of a Saint since there was definitely a halo round it.

For a few minutes she was hopeful.

But as she worked on the canvas she had to be honest with herself and admit that the painting was certainly not by a great master.

In fact, she thought, it was somewhat amateurish.

She pushed the picture to one side impatiently and picked up the other.

She had the feeling they must be a pair.

Therefore as she started to clean away the thick layer of dirt which made the canvas almost black, she was not as optimistic as she had been before.

It was not an easy task.

But she knew it would be a mistake to try and rush it in case she should damage what might turn out to be a valuable painting.

There was a knock on the door and she jumped up eagerly.

Perhaps it was the Earl!

She turned the key and as the door opened she was disappointed to find it was only Watkins.

He came into the room in a conspiratorial way, and did not speak until he had shut the door behind him.

"What is happening?" Thelma asked. "Is His Lordship back?"

" 'E's downstairs with th' Chief Constable," Watkins answered. "An' I'm afraid, Miss Thelma, yer'll be 'avin' luncheon 'ere alone."

Thelma gave a little sigh and he went on:

"Yer wouldn't think they'd 'ave so much to talk about. Th' place be like a Parrot-House wiv everyone tryin' to say somethin' at once!"

Thelma's heart sank.

She knew all the time she had been working on the

picture that her whole body had been tense because she wanted so desperately to see the Earl.

"Is the Chief Constable staying for luncheon?" she asked.

"'Im, an' two or three others, as far as I can make out," Watkins replied. "It be a good thin' I've got some food in th' house!"

Thelma smiled.

"I knew you would be sensible enough to think of that."

"I sends a boy over t' th' farm," Watkins said, "an' another as comes nosing round to th' village with a whole list o' things we requires."

"You will pay for them?" Thelma asked quickly.

Watkins nodded.

"Leave it ter me, Miss! 'Is Lordship's got enough t' think about without doin' the 'ouse-keeping!"

"There has been no trouble over Mr. Mere's death?" Thelma asked a little nervously.

"'Is Lordship 'as told 'em," Watkins replied, "that 'is cousin wanted to bring 'im a present of another tiger for 'is menagerie, but th' animal escaped an' attacked 'im afore 'e could 'and it over."

Thelma smiled.

She herself had already thought that would be the explanation the Earl would give.

"And the animals are all right?" she asked.

"Stuffin' themselves like pigs on that there ox!" Watkins grinned. "An' there's bin so many visitors to stare at 'em, you'd think they was ballet-dancers from Covent Garden!"

Thelma laughed and knew when he left her that Watkins had been trying to cheer her up.

He later brought her luncheon in on a tray, which although it was quite simple was well cooked.

There was a glass of wine from the bottles that had been given to the Earl as a present the previous day.

When she had eaten she went back to work on the picture.

Now, to her surprise, she found that it was not a picture of another Saint, as she had expected, but what was obviously a prayer written in Latin.

She had been taught Latin at School.

And encouraged and helped by her Catholic friend who had told her about St. Jude, she had become quite proficient in it.

As soon as she had cleaned the first line she realised there were several more.

Because she was curious she cleaned the picture completely before she attempted to translate it.

The Latin inscription was now quite clear:

*"GENIBUS NISI TE PRECAMUR*
*UT OMNIA QUAE AMEMUS TUTA SERVENTUR*
*NEVE OCULI IMPROBI UNQUAM VIDEANT*
*QUAE AD DEUM PERTINEANT."*

St. Jude. ∇ 1,2.

Then, although she found some words difficult, she finally wrote down on a piece of paper what she felt sure was a correct translation of the words painted on the canvas.

*"On our knees we plead with Thee*
*That protected all we love will be*
*And evil eyes shall never see*
*What is God's."*

St. Jude. ∇ 1,2.

She read what she had written with pride, then as she looked at the inscription, she was puzzled.

She remembered saying to her Catholic friend:

"Tell me about St. Jude. I do not think he is in our Prayer-Book."

"There is very little known about him," her friend had replied, "except, as I told you, in hopeless causes he will always help those who pray to him."

"There must be something more!" Thelma had persisted.

"He was a friend of Jesus Christ, but as far as I know," her friend answered, "nothing seems to have been written by him."

"Nothing seems to have been written by him!" Thelma repeated now.

She could hear her friend saying this.

And yet here, at the end of the prayer, had been written '*St. Jude V, 1,2*', as if it meant the fifth Chapter of his Epistle, or some Book written by him, and verses one and two.

It was then, with a sudden surge of excitement, Thelma read the Latin again.

> *"Protected all we love will be*
> *And evil eyes shall never see*
> *What is God's."*

She gave a little cry of excitement.

She was sure, quite sure in her mind that she understood what was written and why it had been framed as the second of two pictures.

The first canvas she had tried to clean was a portrait of St. Jude that had hung in the Chapel.

"I am right! I am sure I am right!" she told herself excitedly.

Almost without realising what she was doing, she picked up the picture and carried it towards the door.

Only when she reached it did she remember that she

could not go to the Earl as she longed to do, but must stay locked in her rooms until he sent for her.

Slowly she walked back to the table at which she had been working.

Then she was praying – praying fervently that she was not mistaken, and what the inscription told her was the truth.

It was nearly three o'clock before there was a knock on the door, and when she unlocked it Watkins was outside.

"It's all clear for th' moment, Miss Thelma!" he said. "Yer can come out. 'Is Lordship's waitin' for ye in th' Library."

Thelma gave a little cry of delight.

Picking up the picture and putting it under her arm she ran down the stairs.

Everything was quiet, there was no-one in the hall.

As she glanced out through the open front-door there was nothing to remind her of the horror and the drama of what had taken place last night.

Then because nothing mattered but that she should see the Earl, she started to run down the passage towards the Library.

She threw open the door.

As if he had been waiting for her he turned from the window where he was standing.

He was silhouetted against the sunshine and she thought he looked like Apollo with the light of Greece flaming behind him.

She wanted to run across the room to throw herself into his arms.

Instead, as she suddenly felt shy, she stood just inside the Library door looking at him.

Then as he just looked at her and did not speak she asked in a low voice:

"Is . . everything . . all right?"

"The Chief Constable has accepted my explanation of what occurred," the Earl replied. "There will be no enquiry, no scandal. My cousin Cyril will be buried to-morrow in the family vault."

The Earl spoke in a clear, rather hard voice which made him for the moment seem somehow unapproachable.

Very slowly Thelma walked a little nearer to him, her eyes on his face.

"You will understand," the Earl said, "that in the circumstances it would be best for you to leave here as soon as possible."

"L . leave?"

It was something Thelma had never dreamt he would say to her.

Because not only what he said, but also the almost harsh way he said it came as a shock she put out her hand to hold onto the writing-desk.

Then, without really thinking what she was doing, she put the picture down on it.

"You were on your way somewhere when I invited you to stay the night," the Earl said, "and I think it would be wise, Thelma, now for you to continue your journey, and forget we ever met."

"How can . . you say . . this to . . me?" Thelma asked. "What has . . happened? What . . have I . . done? Why . . have you . . changed?"

The Earl walked away from the window to stand with his back to the empty fireplace.

"I am doing what is best for you," he said after what seemed a long silence.

"How do you . . know it is . . best?" Thelma asked. "How can you send me . . away after . . all that has . . happened?"

There was a little break in her voice on the last word, and the Earl said:

"I am grateful, more grateful than I can ever say, that you saved my life. However, as you are aware, you should not be staying in this house unchaperoned."

116

"Unchaperoned?" Thelma murmured. "Why should you . . think that . . now? Who has been . . talking to . . you? Who has been . . telling you that I . . should be . . chaperoned?"

The Earl's lips curved in a twisted smile.

"Nobody has been talking," he said. "I just made a mistake for which I can only express my deepest regret."

"What . . mistake? What . . are you . . saying?"

She went towards him to stand looking up at him, a piteous expression on her face.

"W . what . . have I done . . wrong?"

"You have done nothing wrong," the Earl replied. "For God's sake, my darling, do not make it any harder than it is already!"

"I . . I do not . . understand," Thelma whispered.

He had called her 'my darling', and she put up her hands to touch him. But he deliberately moved away from her.

"Come and sit down," he said, "and I will try to explain."

Feeling that the world had suddenly turned topsy-turvy and when she least expected it the ceiling had fallen onto her head, Thelma sat down on the sofa.

The Earl did the same but they were not close to each other.

Thelma felt in fact that he was miles away, and what he was saying seemed to come to her through a thick fog.

There was silence until he began:

"When you first came here you told me you were a married woman joining your husband. I knew that was untrue. Then you admitted that you were running away . . ."

"That is . . true!" Thelma said quickly.

The Earl looked away from her across the room.

"I thought then, because you were unattended except by a man-servant, and so well-dressed and riding such an excellent horse, that you had run away from your – lover!"

"M . m . . my lover?" Thelma exclaimed. "How could you . . think or . . imagine such a thing?"

"I admit it was extremely foolish of me," the Earl said, "but because you are so lovely and so utterly desirable, I thought perhaps you could stay with me, and we could be together."

Now there was a deep note in his voice which made Thelma's heart beat frantically.

"That is . . what I . . want," she whispered.

The Earl shook his head.

Then unexpectedly he said in a different tone of voice altogether:

"Tell me the truth – has any man ever possessed you?"

Thelma's eyes opened until they seemed to fill her whole face.

"D . do you . . do you . . mean . . ? No . . of course not . . how could you . . think such a thing?"

"And no man has ever kissed you?"

Now she was shy and the colour rose in her cheeks.

"Only . . you," she whispered.

The Earl rose from the sofa.

"That is what I knew when I kissed you," he said, "and that is why you have to leave me."

"But . . why?" Thelma asked.

"Because I have nothing to offer you, and because, as you are well aware, I cannot keep myself, let alone a wife!"

Thelma gave a gasp.

Then suddenly the room was filled with sunshine and she felt the angels were singing.

"But . . you love . . me?" she questioned in a voice he could hardly hear.

"Of course I love you!" the Earl said roughly. "I love you and I want you, but because I also respect you, and because you are pure and untouched, I have to send you away!"

Thelma felt as if she had suddenly been transported from the depths of darkness and despair into the heart of the sun.

"I love . . you," she said, "and if you . . will . . marry me . . I will look after . . you and help . . you . . and everything . . will be . . all right."

The Earl gave a laugh that was bitter and harsh.

"All right?" he repeated. "In a house that is falling about our ears? In a house in which we cannot afford servants or even the food we must eat to live!"

He walked once again to the window.

"Go away," he said harshly, "and leave me alone in my misery! I cannot stand the torture of thinking of what might have been!"

"But . . listen," Thelma said quickly, "I have . . something to tell you . . something very . . exciting!"

She rose as she spoke to walk towards the picture that was on the table.

As she did so the door of the Library was thrown open and Watkins rushed in.

"Miss Thelma," he said, "it's 'er Ladyship comin' up th' drive!"

Thelma was frozen where she stood.

"It's Dobson drivin'," Watkins said, "an' Jed up beside 'im. I've shut th' front-door to give yer time to 'ide!"

Watkins disappeared and Thelma, with a cry of horror, ran towards the Earl.

"Save me . . hide me!" she pleaded. "If my Stepmother . . finds me, I am . . lost!"

She gripped hold of the lapels of his coat as he stared at her in astonishment, and the tears began to run down her cheeks.

"If she finds . . me here," Thelma went on as the Earl did not speak, "she will . . force me to . . marry her . . lover because he wants my . . money! Oh! Save me . . please . . save me! I will . . die rather than . . marry him."

The Earl put both his hands over hers.

"Is this the truth?" he asked.

"I swear to . . you before . . God that it is . . true . . and she is . . coming to . . take me . . back so that the man with whom she is . . deceiving my . . father can . . spend my . . fortune!"

"And your father has given his consent?"

"Papa will do . . anything she wants . . when he has . . had enough to . . drink!" Thelma faltered.

"And his name?"

"Fernhurst . . Lord Fernhurst! Oh, please . . they will be . . here at any moment . . I must . . hide!"Thelma drew her hands from beneath his and looked around her wildly.

'Go up onto the balcony and lie down," the Earl said quickly. "Do not make a sound, and leave this to me."

Without replying, Thelma ran across the room to climb the spiral stairs up to the balcony.

As she reached it she realised that the flooring of it was a design of flowers and birds fashioned in brass which had darkened until it was almost black.

It hid her completely from anybody down below.

She lay down as the Earl had told her to do on the floor and peeping through the pattern she could see clearly what was happening beneath her.

Slowly the Earl walked to his desk.

Putting the picture she had left there to one side, he took a piece of paper from the leather holder and picked up a quill pen.

As he dipped his pen into the ink the door opened and Lady Fernhurst, followed by Sir Richard Leith, came into the room.

The Earl stared at them with a well-simulated look of surprise.

"You must forgive us for intruding on you," Denise Fernhurst said in her sweetest and most beguiling tone. "We knocked on the front-door, but as no-one answered, we let ourselves into the house."

120

Slowly, as if he suddenly remembered his manners, the Earl rose to his feet.

'You are the Earl of Merstone?" Denise Fernhurst asked.

"I am," the Earl replied, "and perhaps you will tell me who you are and why you are here."

In the same dulcet tones she had used before Lady Fernhurst said as she handed him a newspaper which Thelma knew was a local one:

"This was brought to my notice this morning, and I think you, My Lord, will be able to tell me where I may find my Stepdaughter."

Listening, Thelma held her breath.

She could see her Stepmother very clearly, and she realised she was looking very smart and elegant.

Supposing, she thought with terror, that the Earl considered it was his duty to hand her over.

She looked at Sir Richard Leith, and to her he seemed even more obnoxious than he had when she left home.

There was a smirk on his lips and a look in his eyes which told her all too clearly how eager he was to get his hands on her money.

The Earl was carefully and deliberately reading the paragraph in the newspaper which Lady Fernhurst had handed to him.

It was, he thought, what might have been expected.

The Paragraph was headed:

## "AN UNUSUAL HOME-COMING AT MERSTONE HOUSE"

'The Earl of Merstone returned from the Army of Occupation in France, having been awarded a Medal for Gallantry, to find his magnificient mansion devastated through neglect during the war by those he had left in charge.

His famous menagerie consisting of lions, tigers, as well as

*monkeys and a giraffe, only survived the devastation which*
*had taken place on the Estate by being fed by two faithful*
*servants by slaughtering the deer which have always been a*
*familiar sight in the Park.*

*To save the menagerie now from destruction the Earl had*
*the idea of presenting a Circus for which his friends were*
*invited to pay the unusual sum of one guinea per seat.*

*The Earl himself was the Ring-Master and appeared first*
*to rapturous applause riding a magnificent black stallion*
*called Dragonfly.*

*He was accompanied by a golden-haired, masked young*
*lady riding an equally fine horse who performed the trick of*
*bowing to the audience.*

*Clowns and acrobats as well as the animals amused the*
*appreciative audience for nearly two hours, after which a*
*collection was made which the Earl assured his friends*
*would be spent entirely on the animals' welfare."*

The article continued with a description of the house, the
many generations of Earls who had lived there since the
Earldom was created at the Battle of Agincourt in the
fifteenth century.

The Earl raised his head and looked at Lady Fernhurst.

"My stepdaughter left home riding a white stallion called
*Dragonfly*," she said. "She was accompanied by a groom
who was riding another of my husband's horses by the
name of *Juno*."

Her voice sharpened as she went on:

"I should be grateful, My Lord, if you would send for my
Stepdaughter, who is obviously hiding from us somewhere
in this house."

"I am interested, Lady Fernhurst," the Earl said in a
lofty tone, "to know why your Stepdaughter ran away."

Lady Fernhurst hesitated for a moment.

Then she said with an eloquent little gesture of her
gloved hand:

122

"Thelma is engaged to be married to Sir Richard Leith, who is here beside me. She was at first very happy at the idea, but as often happens to young girls, she suddenly became shy and a little afraid of marriage. I feel sure it is something from which she will recover as soon as I take her home."

The Earl looked at Sir Richard as if for the first time.

Watching him, Thelma thought he could not fail to see how utterly despicable he was and how unpleasant in every way.

But she was not sure, and she began to pray that he would not be deceived by her Stepmother.

"I can assure you, My Lord," Sir Richard said, "that I shall make dear little Thelma very happy, and this girlish quirk will quickly be forgotten."

Still holding the newspaper in his hand the Earl came from behind his writing-desk and walked across the room to stand as he had before in front of the fireplace.

"Perhaps you would like to sit down, Lady Fernhurst," he said, indicating the sofa, "for I think we should discuss this a little further, and decide whether Thelma is really as anxious to be married as you assert."

"Of course she wants to be married!" Lady Fernhurst said angrily. "She is a very lucky girl in that anyone as charming as Sir Richard should offer for her in her first Season. My husband, who unfortunately is not well enough to be here to-day, has given his consent for the marriage to take place as soon as possible."

"Is there any reason why it should be in such a hurry?" the Earl enquired.

He seemed almost to drawl the words.

Watching them Thelma was sure that her Stepmother's temper, which was never far below the surface, was rising at his prevarication.

"I think, My Lord," she said acidly, "you are taking it upon yourself to champion a very unworthy cause. Thelma is a tiresome and very foolish girl, and the sooner she is married and becomes more responsible the better!"

"You may be right," the Earl said a little doubtfully."

"Really, My Lord," Sir Richard interposed, "there does not seem to be any point in talking about this. Lady Fernhurst is here on behalf of her husband. If you will kindly hand her over to us, we need not bother you any further.

"I assure you, Sir Richard," the Earl replied, "it is no bother, and I am as concerned as you are over Thelma's happiness."

"Which is no business of yours!" Lady Fernhurst said rising to her feet. "Will you kindly send a servant to find Thelma? If you refuse to do so I shall reluctantly instruct my servants to seek her out and take her away by force!"

Lady Fernhurst spoke aggressively, and her voice seemed to ring out in the vast Library.

It was with the greatest difficulty that Thelma did not scream out that she would not go.

She covered her mouth with her hand just in case, because she was so frightened, she emitted a sound that would tell them where she was hiding.

Then she heard the Earl say quietly and gravely:

"You have proved to me, Lady Fernhurst and Sir Richard, that Thelma would in fact be very unhappy in your custody. I therefore intend to keep her here with me!"

For a moment Lady Fernhurst was stunned into silence.

Then she lost her temper.

"How dare you say such a thing!" she cried. "How dare you interfere in what is entirely a family matter and has nothing whatsoever to do with you! You will fetch Thelma immediately and, if you do not do so, I will invoke the Law!"

She paused for breath before she went on:

"As Your Lordship must be aware, a father or Guardian has complete control over his daughter, and she will marry whom he pleases!"

"I regret," the Earl said slowly, "that in this instance Lord Fernhurst is too late!"

"What do you mean – too late?" Denise Fernhurst snapped.

"It may come as a surprise to you," the Earl replied, "but in actual fact Thelma is already married – to me!"

# Chapter Seven

For a moment there was a stunned silence.

Then as Lady Fernhurst started to say: "It is illegal!" Sir Richard sprang to his feet.

"You are nothing but a damned fortune-hunter!" he shouted. "How dare you take advantage of a young girl who was riding alone with no-one to protect her! You ought to be shot!"

He seemed to spit the words at the Earl who just stared at him apparently unmoved by his violence.

"Fortune-hunter?" he asked. "What fortune?"

Sir Richard remembered too late that Thelma was not supposed to know about her great-aunt's Will. He looked uncertainly at Lady Fernhurst.

To cover up his mistake Lady Fernhurst repeated almost hysterically:

"It is illegal! Of course it is illegal! I shall take you before the Magistrates and accuse you of abducting an innocent girl and marrying her without her Guardian's consent!"

The Earl smiled in a sarcastic manner and replied quietly:

"I think you would have difficulty, Lady Fernhurst, in proving your point, and most people would consider an Earldom that goes back to the 15th century of more importance than Sir Richard's title, however attractive *you* may find him!"

He emphasised the word '*you*', and it told Lady Fernhurst very clearly that the Earl was aware of Sir Richard Leith's position in her life.

For a moment she was too disconcerted to answer, and the Earl continued in the same tone of voice he had used before;

"I should of course confidently fight any case you may think fit to bring against me and my wife in the House of Lords."

It was then that Lady Fernhurst knew she was defeated.

With a muffled sound of fury she walked towards the door.

When she had nearly reached it, Sir Richard, who had been glowering at the Earl said:

"I would like to call you out for this, Merstone, but I dare say, in view of the state in which you live, you would find it hard to find the bullets!"

"If you do not leave my house immediately," the Earl threatened, "I will throw you out!"

The way he spoke without raising his voice was effective enough to make Sir Richard take a step backwards.

Then with a muttered oath he followed Lady Fernhurst out of the Library, slamming the door behind him.

The Earl merely turned towards the balcony, but for a moment Thelma did not move.

Then as she scrambled to her feet she saw him looking up at her, a smile on his lips.

She gave a little cry of sheer happiness, and hurried down the steps, jumping from the last three into the Earl's arms.

He held her closely against him and she cried incoherently:

"You . . have saved . . me! You have . . saved me! How could you . . have been so . . wonderful! How could . . you have . . understood . . ?"

As she spoke the tears were running down her cheeks but her eyes were shining.

The Earl drew her closer still.

Then he was kissing her passionately, fiercely, demand-ingly, as if he was afraid he might have lost her.

He kissed her until she felt that he carried her up to the stars and nothing else was of any importance because they were together.

"I love . . you!" she murmured. "I . . love you!"

"And I love you, my darling, my precious, but God knows . . "

He was interrupted in what he was about to say as the Library door opened and Watkins came in.

"They've gone, Miss Thelma," he said with satisfaction, "but I finds out what they were about to do – 'er and that nasty piece of work with 'er!"

Moving from the shelter of the Earl's arms, Thelma wiped the tears from her cheeks with the back of her hand.

"They . . have really . . gone?" she asked.

"They went orf lookin' black as thunder!" Watkins said with relish. "Ol' Dobson tells me what they was up to, so just in case there should be any trouble, I takes this from 'em."

He held up a sheet of paper as he spoke and the Earl saw it was a Special Marriage Licence signed by the Archbishop of Canterbury.

Watkins gave it to him saying:

"The coachman tells me, M'Lord, they intended to stop at th' first Church they comes to, an' marry Miss Thelma off to Sir Richard Leith! 'E's a bloke I wouldn't trust no further than I could throw 'im!"

"Nor would I," the Earl agreed, "and it was very sensible of you, Watkins, to take care of this."

He looked down at it, then his eyes twinkled.

"I understand," he said slowly, "that Miss Thelma, as you call her, is handy with a paint brush, so it should not be too difficult to change the name of the bridegroom!"

Thelma gave a little cry.

"You mean . . oh . . tell me what . . you are . . think-ing!"

"I am thinking," the Earl replied, "that Watkins should ride to the village and tell the Vicar that I require him here this evening – at about seven o'clock."

Thelma stared at him, then her face was radiant.

"It will be a very quiet wedding, my darling," the Earl went on, "In my own Chapel but the sooner you are mine the better! Besides, I dislike telling lies!"

Thelma drew in her breath.

"Do you . . really mean . . that?"

"I think it is important that we should be married before your Stepmother and that revolting friend of hers think of some other way of trying to separate us."

Thelma gave a little shiver, and the Earl added quickly:

"Once you are really my wife, I promise you there will be nothing they can do about it."

He put his arm protectively around Thelma as he spoke, and Watkins grinning walked towards the door.

Only as he reached it did Thelma say as if she had suddenly thought of it:

"Wait, wait, Watkins! I want you to help His Lordship!"

Watkins turned round and the Earl looked surprised.

Thelma moving to the desk picked up the picture that she had put there.

With it was the piece of paper on which she had written her translation of the Latin inscription.

"I have something to show you in the Chapel," she said to the Earl, "and please . . let Watkins come too."

"Of course, if that is what you want," he answered.

Carrying the picture, Thelma went ahead of them along the passage beyond the Library and down another staircase which connected the main building with the West Wing.

When they reached the Chapel which she had found the previous day, the sun was coming through the stained glass windows.

Even though many of the panes were cracked and broken, the Chapel was bathed in a golden light and she did not notice the dust and general dilapidation.

She walked up the short aisle to the altar steps.

Then holding the picture in one hand she handed her translation to the Earl.

"Please," she said, "will you read the lines aloud?"

"I will do anything you ask me to do," the Earl replied.

The way he spoke and the love in his eyes made her heart turn over in her breast.

She waited and because he wanted to please her, he read aloud in his deep voice:

*"On our knees we plead with Thee . . "*

Thelma put up her hand to stop him going any further and she said:

"If we were kneeling here on the steps in front of the Communion rail we would be looking at the Sacrament which would be on the altar."

The Earl and Watkins were listening intently.

Then as if he knew what she wanted, the Earl read the next line:

*"That protected all we love will be*
*And evil eyes shall never see*
*What is God's."*

He stopped having finished, and looked at Thelma for explanation.

"Read what is below it," she said.

"St. Jude, V. 1,2" the Earl said.

"I think that the Chancel is five feet from the altar," Thelma told him.

The Earl looked down, then nodded.

"That,' she went on, "'1' indicates the first tombstone

which is immediately below the altar steps."

She pointed down as she spoke.

Both men stared at the huge stone that was directly centred in front of the altar.

It was the tombstone of a mere nobody who had died in 1661.

There was silence. Then the Earl said:

"I do not understand!"

"I believe, in fact I am sure," Thelma said, "that underneath this stone we shall find what the Priests who officiated in this Chapel tried to prevent from falling into the hands of their persecutors."

The Earl stared at her. Then he said:

"The Chapel together with the house which once stood here was built in the reign of Mary Tudor."

"That is what I thought," Thelma said. "Queen Mary, being a Catholic, persecuted the Protestants. Then when her sister Elizabeth came to the throne, being a Protestant, she persecuted the Catholics!"

She saw the expression of hope and excitement which came into the Earl's eyes.

He turned to speak to Watkins, but he was already moving out of the Chapel.

"I knows what yer wants, M'Lord," he said, "an' I'll fetch it!"

The Earl turned back to Thelma.

"Is it possible that you are right?"

As he spoke, he thought that with the sun turning her fair hair into a golden halo no-one could look more beautiful or more spiritual.

'She is like an angel,' he thought.

She had come to him when he was in the depths of despair and had given him hope and faith in the future.

Whether or not there was the treasure she believed they would find in the Chapel, he knew that she was part of him, and he could not live without her.

131

"Whatever I have to do, however hard or degrading it may be," he told himself, "I will keep her with me, and never lose her."

As if she knew what he was thinking, Thelma put out her hand and slipped it into his.

"I am praying," she said softly, "to St. Jude who is the Patron Saint of Hopeless Causes. I cannot believe that he will fail us now."

The Earl raised her hand and kissed it gently.

Then they stood in the sunshine, holding onto each other and both saying silently a prayer.

It was only a few minutes before they could hear Watkins running towards them.

He came into the Chapel with tools which could lift a heavy stone and he also had a garden spade with him.

Without speaking, he handed the Earl a crow-bar and together they lifted the tombstone that formed part of the stone floor.

They did not speak, both men straining every muscle to move what had lain untouched for more than two and a half centuries.

Then as finally they moved it to one side, Thelma held her breath.

As if he thought it was the Earl's right, Watkins handed him the spade and he began to dig.

"'Two feet'!" Thelma whispered, almost beneath her breath.

The dark earth was lifted out onto the floor, then as he dug further, the Earl felt the spade strike something hard.

He put aside the spade and going down on his knees moved the earth with his hand until he could grasp what lay buried.

It seemed to Thelma as if it took an eternity for him to pull what he was holding out of the ground.

First the earth fell away from it, then what she thought

must be the remnants of some cloth with which it had been covered.

The Earl wiped it clean and held it up.

In the rays of the sun shining through the window they could see that it was a chalice.

It was beautifully made of what Thelma was sure was gold, studded with precious stones.

There were huge cabochon rubies, emeralds, diamonds and pearls that had lost their lustre.

Then she was aware that the Earl was looking at it as if he could not believe his eyes.

Gently he put the chalice on the step and reached again into the hole.

As he did so Watkins said:

"I'll be on me way, M'Lord, to th' Vicarage. When I comes back I'll get Walter and Bill to 'elp me clean this place up a bit."

He did not wait for an answer, but was gone as the Earl brought from the dark earth a Paten also of gold and ornamented with jewels.

He set it down beside the chalice, then rose to his feet.

"You were right, my darling!" he said to Thelma. "Everything precious the Chapel possesses is, I am sure, hidden here, and only you could have been clever enough to find it!"

"I think perhaps it was waiting for you all these years," Thelma said, "so that it could be used when it was most needed . . not only for you, but for the . . generations that . . will come . . after you."

The Earl put his arm round her.

"Our sons and our grandsons shall see the house as it was meant to be," he said softly.

He gave a deep sigh as if a heavy burden had been taken from his shoulders.

Then as Thelma looked up at him he knew what she

wanted, and they both knelt down side by side in front of the altar.

It was three hours later that Thelma came from her bedroom to walk down the stairs to where she knew the Earl would be waiting for her.

She thought as she did so that no-one could have a stranger or more wonderful wedding, knowing that God had blessed them beyond their wildest dreams.

She had been busy since they left the Chapel.

The Earl had said:

"We will leave the treasure where it is until to-morrow. More important than anything else at the moment is for you to become my wife."

He had taken Thelma up to her boudoir and put the Special Licence down on the table for her to alter it.

Then he had kissed her until they were both breathless before he left her.

Half an hour later she began to think of her appearance as a bride.

At first she had wished she had something more beautiful to wear for a wedding-gown than the pretty but simple gauze dress that had been attached to *Dragonfly*'s saddle.

But the Earl had brought her a lace veil which he told her had been used by all the Merstone brides for generations.

Also in a leather box there was a diamond tiara which had been locked away in the safe.

It had of course been carefully included in the Inventory because it was entailed, like all the other jewellery, onto the future Earls of Merstone.

The Earl had put on her finger an engagement ring which dated back to the reign of Charles II and clasped round her neck a double collet of diamonds.

Thelma could see it in the portrait of the Countess who had been one of the most beautiful women at the Court of the 'Merrie Monarch'.

134

When she was dressed, she could hardly believe she was not dreaming.

She knew that the Earl, waiting for her, was the hero of her dreams, and even more wonderful than she had imagined any man could be.

"I love him!" she told herself, and hurried because she wanted to make sure he was real.

As she came down the magnificent carved and gilt staircase with its threadbare carpet which she knew they would soon replace, she thought no man could look more handsome.

The Earl was wearing evening clothes, his long-tailed coat covered with decorations and an Order hung round his neck on a red ribbon.

He did not speak, he merely looked at her with such an expression of love in his eyes that she knew nothing mattered so long as they could be together.

Without speaking, the Earl took her by the hand.

They walked quietly and slowly along the corridor which led from the main block to the West Wing.

The Vicar of the Parish, who was also traditionally the Earl's Private Chaplain, was waiting for them.

When they entered the Chapel, Thelma knew that only Watkins could have transformed it so quickly.

The sun had sunk but there was a faint glow left in the sky outside.

The altar was bathed in the light of many candles and the brilliance of them disguised any short-comings of dust and dilapidation still existing in the Chapel.

Somewhere Watkins had found a white altar cloth which was heavily embroidered with gold thread.

Walter and Bill must have picked every flower that was available in the garden.

The tombstone had been replaced and there was a red carpet covering it which reached almost to the door of the Chapel.

As Thelma and the Earl knelt down in front of the altar she knew that beneath them lay enough wealth to make him feel they were equals.

The fact that she had any money of her own was unimportant.

At the same time, she knew they could now make the house perfect in every way, and the Alms-Houses, the Pensioners' cottages and the Schools on the Earl's estate would be a model for the whole country.

He put the wedding-ring which had been his mother's on her finger and they knelt while the Chaplain blessed them.

Thelma knew that she would dedicate her whole life to her husband and children and she prayed that they would love her.

She would also, she thought, be eternally grateful that she had been saved by St. Jude from having to marry a man she hated.

"Thank you, thank you!" she said silently.

She knew now that St. Jude would be a special Saint not only for herself and the Earl, but also for their children.

As they rose to their feet the Earl lifted her hand and kissed it.

"My wife!" he said softly.

She knew it was a kiss of dedication and he thought as she did.

They went from the Chapel into the Drawing Room and the Chaplain drank their health in a glass of wine, then returned to the village.

As soon as they were alone, the Earl said:

"We have been married for quite a long time, my precious one, and I have not yet kissed you!"

Thelma lifted her lips to his.

"Kiss me . . please . . kiss me," she begged. "I did not know until last night that a . . kiss could be so . . wonderful."

He kissed her and she felt as if her whole body melted

into his, and it was impossible for them ever to be divided.

Then as they moved apart Watkins came in to say:

"Dinner is served, M'Lady!"

Thelma blushed because this was the first time she had been addressed as a Countess.

They went in to dinner hand-in-hand, and found that once again Watkins had been busy.

The table was decorated with white flowers and the food he had cooked for them was simple, but delicious.

"To-morrow," the Earl said, "we can begin to plan exactly how many people we require in the house to wait on us."

Thelma laughed.

"I think the best thing we can do is to leave all that to Watkins. He will enjoy taking charge of the household while we plan how we can redecorate the rooms."

The Earl put out his hand and she laid hers in it.

"For the moment," he said, "I can think of nothing but how much I love you!"

"That is what I want you to say," she answered. "At the same time, there are so many exciting things that we can do, and I know you will want to extend your menagerie."

"It had crossed my mind!" the Earl admitted.

"We will make it the best menagerie in the country!" Thelma vowed.

She paused, then looking at her husband a little shyly she said:

"I am hoping . . perhaps we might find . . some of the special animals . . ourselves."

"What you are saying," the Earl replied, "Is that you want to travel abroad!"

"It would be wonderful if I was with you."

"Then that is what we will do," he said. "But first we have to make this a home to come back to, and be quite certain that the people who belong here no longer suffer as they have done since I left them in the charge of Cyril."

Thelma gave a little cry.

"Do not think of him! We must not speak about him!"

The Earl smiled before he said quietly:

"Perhaps in some strange and twisted manner, it was because he was responsible for my giving a Circus that you came into my life."

"That is true," Thelma said, "for if I had not seen the Big Top and the tiger being led back to his cage on a lead, I should have just looked at the house, then ridden on."

"It was Fate," the Earl replied. "When you came into the tent I thought you were not only the most beautiful person I had ever seen, but also I felt instinctively within myself that you meant something very special to me."

"I felt the same," Thelma said, "but I could not put it into words. I only knew that I did not want to . . leave you."

His fingers tightened on hers.

"That is something you will never do."

Their eyes met and after a moment he said:

"Come, my darling. I want to be closer to you than we can be here, and there is no-one to be surprised if we go to bed early."

Thelma laughed.

They went up the stairs with their arms around each other.

Because her own room was in darkness she knew where she would sleep to-night.

It might be in need of paint, new curtains and another carpet.

Yet in the candlelight the Earl's bed-room was very impressive with its huge four-poster bed, its crimson velvet hangings and the carved and gilded posts.

It had served generation after generation of the Earl's ancestors.

Again Watkins had provided flowers which now scented the room with their fragrance.

138

Thelma went to the window to pull back the curtains.

The stars were like diamonds in the sky, and the moonlight later filled the room with its silver light.

Thelma moved a little closer to the Earl and pressed her lips against his shoulder.

"I love you!" she whispered.

"You are quite certain of that?" he asked. "I have not hurt or frightened you, my darling?"

"I feel as if you took me through the Gates of Heaven! I had no idea that one could feel such rapture and ecstasy, and still be alive!"

The Earl drew in his breath.

"I adore you!" he said. "How is it possible I should have been so lucky as to find you at the very moment when I needed you most? I was in despair, and almost wishing that a French bullet had killed me!"

Thelma gave a little cry.

"How can you say . . anything so wicked . . so wrong?"

"You changed everything," the Earl said, "and as you say, only in a dream or a Fairy-Story could we be introduced through a Circus!"

"A Circus for Love!" Thelma breathed. "You arranged it because you loved your animals. Then when you were so kind to me and asked me to stay the night, I think, although we were not yet aware of it, that it was love."

The Earl tightened his arms round her but he did not interrupt and Thelma went on:

"I wanted to help you. I felt sure there must be . . something in the house that was not entailed and would enable you to . . live as you . . should! It was love that made me . . pray to St. Jude."

The Earl's lips were on her forehead, moving gently against the softness of her skin.

"It was love which brought me the treasure which lies in the Chapel," he said, "and it was love which brought me a much greater treasure, one that is mine for all eternity and one I shall never lose and no-one shall take from me!"

He pulled her closer as he said:

"You are mine, my precious, mine completely and absolutely! I swear I would kill anyone who tried to take you from me!"

"I am yours," Thelma said, "and I am no longer . . afraid that I might be forced into . . marriage with . . somebody like . . Sir Richard!"

"Forget him!" the Earl said. "Again in a strange manner he was responsible for your running away and that brought you to me."

Thelma gave a little laugh.

"That is true, so life is really a Circus and, in its own way, very exciting!"

"That is what you are," the Earl said gently. "You excite me to madness! At the same time, my precious, I worship you! You are everything I want as a wife, and thought I would never find. You are everything any man could want as the mother of his children."

Thelma buried her face against him.

Then in a small voice he could hardly hear she said:

"I did not . . know that making love was . . so wonderful. Do you . . think you have . . given me a . . baby?"

The Earl smiled.

"Perhaps," he said, "but of course, we can always try again, to make sure!"

He drew her still closer and his lips were on hers.

Then as she felt a wild excitement rising within her and knew too that she excited the Earl, she pulled his head down to hers.

She felt as if the fire on his lips was answered by a fire on hers.

"I love . . you! I love . . you!" she wanted to say, but the Earl was carrying her up on a shaft of moonlight into the sky.

The stars were all around them, and as an ecstasy rose within her they were in her mind, her breasts and her heart.

She and the Earl had gone through danger, disaster and fear to find each other, but now she was safe; safe in the arms of the man she loved.

"I want you," the Earl said hoarsely. "I want you, my precious! Give me yourself. I want you completely!"

"I am . . yours . . all yours," Thelma whispered. "Please . . love me."

Then as he swept her into Heaven itself she knew their love came from God, was part of God, and was theirs for all eternity.

## OTHER BOOKS BY BARBARA CARTLAND

*Romantic Novels, over 400, the most recently published being:*

A Caretaker of Love
Secrets of the Heart
Riding to the Sky
Lovers in Lisbon
Love is Invincible
The Goddess of Love
And Adventure of Love
A Herb for Happiness
Only a Dream
Saved by Love
Little Tongues of Fire
A Chieftain Finds Love
The Lovely Liar
The Perfume of the Gods
A Knight in Paris
Revenge is Sweet
The Passionate Princess
Solita and the Spies
The Perfect Pearl
Love is a Maze
The Dream and the Glory (In aid of the St. John Ambulance Brigade)

*Autobiographical and Biographical:*
The Isthmus Years 1919-1939
The Years of Opportunity 1939-1945
I Search for Rainbows 1945-1976
We Danced All Night 1919-1929
Ronald Cartland (With a foreword by Sir Winston Churchill)
Polly – My Wonderful Mother
I seek the Maraculous

*Historical:*
Bewitching Women
The Outrageous Queen (The Story of Queen Christina of Sweden)

The Scandalous Life of King Carol
The Private Life of Charles II
The Private Life of Elizabeth, Empress of Austria
Josephine, Empress of France
Diane de Poitiers
Metternich – The Passionate Diplomat

*Sociology:*
You in the Home
The Fascinating Forties
Marriage for Moderns
Be Vivid, Be Vital
Love, Life and Sex
Vitamins for Vitality
Husbands and Wives
Men are Wonderful
Etiquette
The Many Facets of Love
Sex and the Teenager
The Book of Charm
Living Together
The Youth Secret
The Magic of Honey
The Book of Beauty and Health
Keep Young and Beautiful by Barbara Cartland and Elinor Glyn
Etiquette for Love and Romance
Barbara Cartland's Book of Health

*Cookery:*
Barbara Cartland's Health Food Cookery Book
Food for Love
Magic of Honey Cookbook
Recipes for Lovers
The Romance of Food

*Editor of:*
"The Common Problem" by Ronald Cartland (with a preface by
the Rt. Hon. the Earl of Selborne, P.C.)
Barbara Cartland's Library of Love
Barbara Cartland's Library of Ancient Wisdom

"Written with Love" Passionate love letters selected by Barbara Cartland

*Drama:*
Blood Money
French Dressing

*Philosophy:*
Touch the Stars

*Radio Operetta:*
The Rose and the Violet (Music by Mark Lubbock) Performed in 1942.

*Radio Plays:*
The Caged Bird: An episode in the Life of Elizabeth Empress of Austria Performed in 1957.

*General:*
Barbara Cartland's Book of Useless Information with a Foreword by the Earl Mountbatten of Burma.
(In aid of the United World Colleges)
Love and Lovers (Picture Book)
The Light of Love (Prayer Book)
Barbara Cartland's Scrapbook
(In aid of the Royal Photographic Museum)
Romantic Royal Marriages
Barbara Cartland's Book of Celebrities
Getting Older, Growing Younger

*Verse*:
Lines on Life and Love

*Music:*
An Album of Love Songs sung with the Royal Philharmonic Orchestra.

*Film:*
The Flame is Love